BEWARE OF FLIGHT ATTENDANT

CACTUS MOLONEY

This book is dedicated, with much love, to my clever mama.

The killings already happened~

A DOG IS A MAN'S BEST FRIEND

A CAR MIGHT HAVE HIT me.

I had crap for memories before the dog pound. The flyspecked leftovers of my past were all that remained in my dreams.

I awoke dazed and confused, in the middle of the street, with my body stretched across the two yellow lines, quickly standing to shake myself off before darting away at a sprint. Lickety-split, the tender pads of my paws became painfully raw on the stovetop pavement. No matter, I continued, searching the scorched New Mexico desert suburb. I was chasing someone; who was a mystery to me. The memory hanging in front me like the lure of greyhound's artificial rabbit rail—if I could just grasp it.

When my searing paws could take no more, I spotted two small girls giggling in delight, jumping through the sprinklers watering their lawn. They flaunted little ruffled swimsuits, dancing with the water rotation splashing them in the cool, green, grass yard. It created an oasis from the brutal sunshine, surrounding cactus, rock gardens, and black asphalt roads, with waves of heat dancing at eye level.

The grass became a carpeted reprieve from the stinging burn. Immediately, I dropped onto my back, twisting my body against the welcoming earth, greedily absorbing its luxurious comfort. Water sprinkles tapped fresh droplets against my exposed pink tummy. It smelled alive.

I smiled from ear to ear.

"Hee hee," the small blond girl started laughing at me. "You're a happy doggy."

I jumped to my feet to greet her, standing eye to eye with her and another little person the same size.

"Who are you?" Asked the little girl, sporting long brown drenched pigtails, dressed in a suit the color of lemons, with hip fringe, and a cartoon princess stretched across her extended stomach. "You have golden eyes, pup."

I felt a sudden burst of energy, jetting from my crouched position, to make quick circles around the small people, flying through the sprinklers.

"Hee hee, yay," I heard the blond girl laughing loudly. "Eeew doggy—he is sooo cute!"

"Oh my God!" An adult woman blurted from nearer the two-floor stucco house.

I halted, regarding the woman's excited voice curiously. Frozen as still as an ice sculpture with my head cocked to the side, making sure I didn't miss any cues. I blinked the water droplets from my eyes. The motherly woman was holding a tray of Red Delicious apples, with creamy peanut butter, and cheese sticks. I smelled all three simultaneously.

"Where did you come from?" She asked me. "You are the biggest silver dog I ever saw."

In response to her friendly tone, I decided to make even faster, tighter, circles around the girls, until I rolled on to my back—sliding to a stop in front of them—my belly again exposed to show my submission. I wiggled by body.

Pet me, I willed them.

The mother set down the tray of food, with it clinking against the small concrete table. Her rubber sandals chirped like a squeaky toy, walking her through the sprinklers, fully dressed in a t-shirt and jean shorts to squat down next to the girls and me. Reaching out, she rubbed my readily available pink-skinned, white-furred belly. Her hands felt cool. I could feel the little girls' saturated fingers gently rubbing behind my ears.

"Can we keep him mommy?"

"No way babe...the last thing we need is a dog," the mother said.

"Please mama!!!"

"Babe this dog belongs to someone else...he looks well cared for...see how he has a blue bandana around his neck."

She felt around the bandana with her clammy hands, searching for something.

"But he doesn't have a tag—darn it."

"What's that?" The blond girl asked.

"A tag has the owner's phone number or address. I would call them to let them know where their dog is. They're probably worried sick."

"We can take care of him mommy," the pig-tailed girl encouraged her mother. "Until his parents find him."

"I'm going to call Animal Control, girls. They need to come collect him, so they can help him to find his mommy or daddy."

Watching the girls, I thought about how this would be a great place to live. I snuggled closer to them, wiggling my body with happiness and joy.

"He's hurt, mommy," the pigtailed girl mused, softly touching my hindquarters with her tiny wrinkled fingers.

She poked around the throbbing area that I hadn't felt

until now. *Ouch.* "He has blood on his leg and on his face mommy."

The mother called for the girls.

"Come eat your snack!"

I followed behind them to the concrete table, lying down between the sweeties, with my white-tipped paws crossed formally in front of me. As I had hoped, my politeness paid off when they shared their snack with me. I think cheese and peanut butter are my favorite foods. The peanut butter stuck to the roof of my mouth, forcing me to keep licking at it, smacking my chops in bliss. Saliva strings drooled from my lips to stroke the grass.

After snack time, a white truck pulled into the driveway. It had several air-conditioned dog kennels on the tail end. I guessed it was time to go. A man in a tan uniform stepped from behind the vehicle, holding a long pole with a rope attached to the end. *Yikes.* I needed to play this right, in order to not get roughed up. I sat perfectly still between the girls. They were crying. Leaning my heavy head against the blond girl's leg, I tried to comfort her. I raised my eyes to see her sobbing face. I felt her sadness as if it were my own. It was.

"Mommy, no!" The blond girl blubbered, "Don't let that man take him."

The mom approached the dogcatcher and was speaking to him. I watched as he set down the pole and began walking towards me with his hand stretched out in front of him to offer me a whiff. Sniffing at his palm, I smelled a dozen different dogs, and antiseptic cleaner from the dog pound. I could smell nothing mean about him.

He patted me behind my cartilage thick ears, and then tapped his leg for me to follow. As requested, I trailed behind him with my rejected head hanging low. He opened the door to the kennel and drummed the open space with his hand. Not missing the beat, I jumped in and lay my head between my white paws.

My first day at the dog shelter, the man in tan walked me to the veterinarian's office, located behind a door at the end of the hallway. It was the longest walk of my life. I was so scared. The noise was earsplitting. Dogs were leaning against the metal gates, some were howling, others were giving me a sorrowful parting, as they scratched a goodbye at the empty air.

"It's just for a check-up, buddy," the man in tan informed me. "They're going to fix you."

I made it out of the vet's office alive that day—not fully intact—the once bulging sack between my legs had been reshaped to form a saggy-skinned ineffective waste. The purebred bloodline butchered.

I was only in the shelter for a few more days before Cindy came to rescue me. I had never met her. Putting her hand out to introduce herself, she then ran it down my rigid back and then gently inspected the muscles of my thighs. Her lips pulled into a smile. She was impressed.

"I'm going to train you to be a service animal," she said gleefully.

I was game—anything to get me off death row. I had watched too many dogs take the final walk. I had begun joining the other mutts in the clamorous farewell chorus—bidding our comrades adios—never to see them again. I knew the unfortunate ones hadn't been adopted or lost their balls.

The new kennel at Cindy's had a comfortable bed and better food. It also had her assistant Lenny. He was a real tail-dropper. Not a nice guy. He smelled of Pall Malls and booze. He had served time in prison for domestic abuse and larceny. The tattoos covering his body told a history of gang violence.

Cindy characterized Lenny as a "trained professional," with an adept's understanding of dog behavior.

"He holds the proper qualifications to train service animals," she said. "Acquired through a dog-training program made available during a prison stint. He is a passionate Pitbull enthusiast."

"You are a Pitbull," she said petting me behind my ears.

Cindy didn't know that Lenny was two-faced. He followed her dog-training regimen when she was around. While she watched, he would encourage the dogs with positive words, "Good job dog," supplying us with nibbles of cheese to reward our efforts. When she left for the day, the man would turn darker and surlier with every swig he took from the flask of vodka hidden in his blue Dickey's pants pocket.

Lenny didn't abuse me as much as the others. I always followed his orders. He chose to focus his efforts elsewhere. I don't think the other dogs, Fred and Songbird, meant to disobey. They genuinely couldn't understand Lenny's drunken ramblings.

I had been at Cindy's kennel for approximately two weeks; it was dusk when everything became smudged in black shadows. Lenny let us outside for our nightly sniff and leak. I trotted to the far side of the agility course to urinate on my favorite tree. The dead yellow patches of grass that I had killed with my piss stood out brightly in the reflected moonlight. Camouflaged by the tree's obscure overhang, I listened as Lenny slurred a command to Fred.

"Go shit!"

Fred didn't move a muscle. He was doing his best to

obey Lenny's command; clearly thinking the trainer had said *Sit*.

"Get out there you stupid fucking mutt!" He yelled at Fred, "Shit!"

Fred just sat there. I could feel the tension building in Lenny, like the buzz of an electrical wire.

Then, Lenny started kicking Fred in the ribs and stomach. The large German shepherd could have been fierce, but the poor guy was a pussycat. Lenny continued to kick at the big dog. Fred would grunt with each whack, until he cried out in pain. I felt helpless watching this happen from my darkened hideout.

"I see your creepy golden eyes, you bastard," he hollered to me where I stood in the dark.

He stumbled around the yard yelling, "Kennel up, you freaks."

Lenny opened the door from outside to allow the three of us to pass into the concrete corridor, leading to our individual cells. Along the right side were eight air-conditioned kennels, expanding the length of the building. On the left side, a wall of windows overlooked the agility park. Concrete partitions separated the rooms; with the chain-link gates propped open, allowing us to slip past the doors, into our individual units. I could hear Fred breathing hard through his pain, as he limped into his space.

Lenny kicked at Songbird when she entered her kennel. She attempted to dodge him with her tail tucked between her hind legs.

"Bitches get stitches," he said, seething at her.

Clink, Lenny closed the beautiful Rottweiler's cage.

Clink, Lenny closed Fred's kennel. Fred's tall ears had collapsed behind his head in defeat.

Clack, Lenny closed the door to my cell, but I noticed

the sound was distinctly different from the *clink* of the other gates.

Sitting on my bed, I waited for Lenny to turn off the buzzing fluorescent hallway lights. My nubby ears perked to listen for the door leading to the offices to shut behind him. Standing from my bed, I moseyed over to the chain-link gate to inspect the latch. Giving it a small push with my scrunched jet muzzle. *Creak.* The chain-link gate swung outward into the hallway.

Stepping into the hallway, I heeded my disguise; my dark silver fur blended with the gray concrete floors and gunmetal gates. The windowed door to the offices was at the end of the hall. I knew how to open doors. This one had a lever handle. I gently hopped my front feet onto the door, sliding my white paws against the lever, dropping my feet back down to the ground. I hadn't bumped the handle with my front foot hard enough the first time. So, I tried again, walking upright on my back feet, aiming both of my front paws at the handle. Trying to be quiet not to alert Lenny. I tapped the handle with my paws again and heard the *click*. The door cracked open just enough for me to fit my mug in the opening, pulling the door towards me, I squeezed my body through. The door *clicked* shut behind me. I took mindful steps to hide the tapping sound of my toenails against the concrete floor.

Lenny was still in the building. I listened to his shoes squeaking on the concrete, dancing back and forth in the front lobby area. Peering around the corner, I discovered the sound was Lenny mopping the floor. I noticed headphones covered his ears; with the angry music blasting his eardrums, he couldn't hear me.

Pausing to place the mop against the welcome desk, he reached into his pants pocket to pull out the flask.

Unscrewing the lid with his jailhouse tattooed fingers, the left middle three fingers spelled P-I-T, the right fingers showed B-U-L, he tilted his head back and polished off the remaining vodka.

Lenny was standing in a puddle of water.

I thought about Fred crying alone in his cell.

Grrrrrrrr.

The rumbling thunder rolled from deep within me. My chest and throat became a vibrating electrical storm surging at Lenny. I was a force to reckon with.

Lenny stopped mid-reach for the mop, turning his body to face the tremor. I wanted him to see me. He was off balance and drunk. Locking his bloodshot, baffled eyes with my own appearing as two glowing orbs hovering in the dark corner. I was snarling. My lips curled back to expose my bright white fangs. My mouth was raining saliva from the smell of his anxiety.

"Hey, dog," Lenny squinted his eyes to better to see me with. "How the fuck did you get..."

I felt calm. I was in control. The fountain of drool continued pouring from my mouth.

Lenny had told me, "You are a product of selective breeding. Humans designed you by selecting the best genes."

Beginning with my wolf forefathers, he said, I was stronger and smarter than the animals that came before me.

Rearing back into my powerful hind legs I blasted forward. My front paws punching him in the chest—one hundred and fifty pounds of "genetically superior" bulk muscle. His feet slipped in the puddle of soapy water, causing him to tumble backwards from the impact, cracking the nape of his neck hard against the Welcome Desk.

The *crunch* sound of his spinal cord snapping was satisfying. The trainer dropped to the ground with a sliding thud. Blood began pooling around his head to form a cone of shame. His eyes remained locked on mine—blinking rapidly—blood gurgling from his open mouth. Less than a minute later, his eyes stopped blinking and remained open. Fixed on me. The offensive music was beating against his ears. The band continued to rage for the lifeless audience.

I slowly backed up, taking measured steps with my white paws, making sure not to get messy. I didn't want to leave prints behind as evidence that I had been there. I backed into the dark hallway, dropping my body onto the cold concrete to watch Lenny die. His head wound continued to gush large amounts of blood, mixing with the sudsy mop water.

Sitting as still as a gargoyle statue on the gray concrete, I waited for any sign of movement from Lenny for some time —nothing.

I was dog-tired and felt like joining my mates in the comforts of my kennel. The office door was even easier returning, with only a push bar across the middle of the door. I jumped up and bumped my hefty shoulder against the bar. I wasn't concerned about the noise this time. It popped open, allowing me easy access to the kennels. I listened to door close behind me with a *click*. Trudging past Songbird, I could see she lay mostly hidden in the dark cage, her kind black eyes looking back at me with concern, one light-brown eyebrow raised curiously.

Fred was sleeping fitfully in the next cell, his legs kicking sporadically. He wouldn't need to hide from Lenny anymore. Finding my own kennel, I wrapped my teeth around the chain-link gate, and pulled it shut with a *clink*.

Plopping down on my soft bed, I said to Fred, "You are safe now, my friend."

DRIVING over the speed limit heading for Doggy Stiles Training Center, Cindy came around the corner, hitting the curb with a hard jolt. Her favorite worn cassette blasted Melissa Etheridge's *Come to my Window,* out the open windows of her dark blue 1996 Ford Explorer.

The inside of the Explorer was covered in short brown fur. Tiny brown dog hair quills carpeted the floor—each impossible to vacuum. A few difficult-to-remove, short brown hairs didn't matter much, when the entire 4x4 was covered in the gamut of all dog hair ever created: long white hairs, short black, brown, red and blond hairs of every length. Fur balls were knitted to the edges of the seats, congregating in all the corners of the carpeted flooring. The windows were smeared with dog slime, snout kisses, and licks from their pink tongues.

"It smells like wet dog in here!" she hollered at her mutts in the back of the "Mongrel Mobile."

She parked the Explorer in a space at the side of the training center, making sure to leave the handicapped spot in the front available.

"Ready kids?"

She cast her gold-speckled brown eyes into the review mirror to admire Zeek; her black long-haired Pyrenees mix, who she had adopted from the Humane Society shelter several years prior. Luke sat next to him; an intelligent three-year-old black German shepherd rescue dog, who assisted Cindy with the training sessions. On the passenger seat, sat her two, shining fawn-colored Dachshunds, Bonnie and Clyde. Clyde was licking the inside of Bonnie's open mouth, giving her sharp teeth a polished sheen.

Rehabilitating animals was something Cindy was passionate about. She was living the dream, owning her very own dog school for rehabilitation and service dog training, in her hometown of Albuquerque, New Mexico. "There is no such thing as a broken dog," Cindy said, believing any dog could be fixed with patience, time, training and love.

"Come Bonnie...come Clyde," she commanded the wieners.

Clyde happily complied, with Bonnie following behind reluctantly. She opened the Explorer's back hatch; it was covered in dog sticker regalia. Cute stick-on paw prints ran from one side of the explorer to the next. Bumper stickers plastered the vehicle: *Honk to see my WEINER, I heart my shelter dog, Pitbulls are for hugs—Not thugs,* and *Flop don't Crop.* Shadow stickers of her dog family could be found on the rear window, with the family line ending with two human stick figures, representing herself and her wife, Tamara.

Tamara was an ash blond, who stood four inches taller than Cindy at five-foot-nine in her bare feet. Her bone thin body lived in yoga pants and soft, organic cotton, cropped yoga shirts, revealing her sharp hip bones and exposed ribs.

Cindy's muscular squat body seemed exaggerated when she stood next to her paradoxical wife. With her short, mousy hair trimmed close at the sides and spiked tall at the crown of her head. Tamara told her the style gave height to her round face. A chain connected her leather wallet to knee length, tan cargo shorts, along with a revolving white or black *Doggy Stiles* logotype t-shirt. She kept strong from her commitment to the arduous labor required by a dog trainer; cleaning the dog kennels, hiking with the dogs, playing fetch at Sandia Lakes, and running the service dog intensive training course.

Most of Tamara's time was spent managing the yoga studio and teaching Bikram classes twice daily. She complained about her clients regularly.

"I can't believe that bitch said *Om* louder than me again!"

"Today a lady slipped on a man's sweat during hot yoga, while holding Virabhadra.... She signed a waiver...so we're not liable."

Tamara had demonstrated the pose with perfect balance, holding her toned arms out to each side. She appeared to be flying while balancing on one leg.

"You know the fierce pose. So, while balancing on one foot—I guess she slipped in this guy's sweat—landing on her face and breaking her nose. Blood spurted everywhere. We had to close the classroom down and disinfect the mess. The woman acted like it was our fault!"

Interrupting the yogi rant, Cindy changed the subject to dogs.

"Tammy you aren't going to believe what I saw at Sandia Lakes. One of those 'carbon leash' kind of lazy owners, running the dog next to their vehicle," Cindy would become haughty thinking about all the ignorant dog owners.

"I always give the dogs my full, and undivided attention on walks."

"Do you have any idea how many owners have 'accidentally' run over their own dogs?" She asked Tamara rhetorically, making quotation marks with her stumpy chewed fingernails.

Tamara had tried to induct herself into the dog business, bringing Cindy grand ideas she thought would help build clientele. After she had presented the off the wall idea to offer 'Yoga in the Dog Park,' Cindy had had enough.

"You keep your nose in your own dog business Tamara," she scolded her wife. "I don't tell you how to run the yoga studio...or how to pose like a cat."

Cindy offered basic dog-training classes for the community, on Wednesday nights at 6pm; walk INS were welcome. However, she chose to focus the majority of her energy and time on the monumental task of training service dogs.

"It takes a dog park to raise a puppy," she would tell clients.

———

Blue skies and a cool desert breeze welcomed Cindy to the training center. A new wooden business sign hung above the center, the background was painted bright orange, with red-stenciled lettering *Doggy Stiles Training Center*. In the right-hand corner, a pointed-eared German shepherd was painted leaping over a stocky American Pitbull Terrier. Today, she was going to pair a person with Buster, her most recently trained and licensed diabetic alert dog.

"What a day!" she exclaimed to her mutt pack.

Smiling, she unlocked the double glass doors, and

walked in the entryway, flipping on the lights. It smelled of antiseptic cleaner. Even a month after the accident, she continued to hold her breath each time she flipped on the lights.

She hoped she would never again witness a scene as horrifying as the day she found her assistant Lenny lying dead in a pool of blood and soapy water, his headphones still blasting music amidst the grisly scene.

A clean stark lobby greeted her; she exhaled with relief. Walking over to the front desk, she booted up the computer, and then ambled back to her office to start a pot of coffee. She could hear the dogs' friendly barks coming from their kennels in response to her movements.

The dogs were familiar with the sounds of her morning routine. They were telling her it was time for breakfast. She headed down the hallway, opening the windowed door facing into the boarding kennel. Rarely did Cindy have all eight kennels full to capacity. She wouldn't be able to give the attention needed to train so many service dogs, even if she still had her assistant's help.

Lenny, may he rest in peace, had realized his passion for working with animals in a prison Pitbull training-program. He had been a vital resource for training the dogs. Gifted with the intuitive ability to sniff out aggressive animals. He had the knack for finding easily trainable dogs, those possessing the qualities required of a service animal.

Cindy was a firm advocate for adopting dogs from the pound, pushing people never to purchase animals from breeders.

"Too many good dogs need a home," she would tell her clients. "Raising dogs for the sake of making money could turn people's good intentions bad. With inbreeding and puppy mills...adopting a shelter dog is the only way to go."

Before Lenny's accident, they would take off on road trips, seeking out hidden canine candidates by scouring the states surrounding New Mexico. They would check Craigslist, the Humane Society, and numerous dog pound and rescue websites throughout Utah, Arizona, Colorado and Texas. Sometimes they would drive ten hours, across the flat yellow, sandy desert reservations, passing the newer modular homes build beside the traditional rounded Navajo hogans of the Native American people. They would witness packs of stray dogs, clearly inflicted with distemper, parvovirus, infested with mange and ringworm, roaming the reservation wastelands. Cindy suffered the heartbreak from driving through the Third World—slap dab in the middle of the USA—anything to save a dog with potential. Most of the time they would return home empty handed. Cindy was looking for dogs that did not bark or cause a nuisance; the dog needed leash understanding, good behavior, discipline, basic prior training, and an acceptance of strangers. It was a lot to ask from a shelter dog, and that was just the beginning, before the intensive training began.

"Hola, buenos días, Buster," Cindy greeted her newest canine achievement.

Buster was an enormous muscular silver Blue Nose Pitbull Terrier, with a white apron chest, velvet black nose, and knobby-cropped ears. His entire wide-stance body wagged to compensate for his stubby tail. He welcomed her with a Cheshire Cat sly grin from ear to ear.

She hadn't had to go far to find Buster, he had been held at a shelter in Los Ranchos, a suburb outside of Albuquerque. The shelter rang Doggy Stiles Training Center to inform Cindy of an exceptionally obedient Pitbull, scheduled for euthanizing due to its breed and overcrowding in the shelter.

"We need to find him a home within the next twenty-four hours," the shelter worker had explained. "This dog has a sweet disposition, and a clear understanding of hand commands, plus he's gorgeous."

Cindy rushed to the suburban shelter to assess the dog. She found the abandoned animal sitting calmly on the shelter's cold-cemented kennel floor, his white paws positioned attentively in front of him. The arrested dogs in the cells surrounding him continued barking and whining, causing a roaring echo of chaos in the cemented chamber; it was an ideal first meeting place to assess an animal.

"Sit," she commanded the shelter dog.

The silver dog continued standing, smiling up at her with its piercing yellow eyes. Her heart dropped.

"You told me he knew commands?"

"Try using your hands to signal him and see what happens," suggested the curly-haired shelter worker.

Cindy put her hand out, motioning for the dog to *Sit*. He immediately complied. She motioned her hand toward the floor. The dog obeyed by lying down. She rolled her hand over and he did the same. Reaching into her fanny pack, she pulled out a chicken nibble to treat the dog for his tricks from the pouch around her waist. It held the reward treats, along with other doggy paraphilia: green plastic poop bags, the dog clicker training system, an additional leash, and her keys. She kept her phone in a leather holster on her hip, alongside her trusty Leatherman.

These were all fun games, but she wondered why he hadn't understood her verbal commands?

"Is he deaf?" she asked the uniformed man.

"Maybe his previous owner was mute...or maybe the dog speaks a different language?"

She motioned for the massive dog to stand back up.

"Sientate," she commanded the silver stray.

He immediately plopped down on his backside. She again handed him a small bite of chicken

"Quedate," she held her palm out, in a stop motion, as she backed out of the kennel.

The dog stayed. She took measured steps, backing down the hallway; dogs on each side were barking and jumping against their kennel's chain-link gates. High-pitched small scruffy dogs yipped, and low double bass barks erupted from each side, then howling from a sad-eyed Bagel, a Basset Hound-Beagle mix, commenced. She waited, counting to thirty.

"Four, five, six...twenty-eight, twenty-nine... aqui," she commanded the dog, calmly, not changing the timbre of her voice.

Buster came bolting from his kennel, sliding around the corner, trying to catch his footing as his nails skidded along the smooth concrete floor. His speed and urgency caused his lips to slip back into a goofy grin. He touched her hand with his wet nose. Sitting at her side, he acted amused, beaming up at her.

"Is he always so eager to please?" She asked the dogcatcher, who was standing out of the way, near the door.

"This dog is at your beck and call," the curly haired man responded. "Usually with *pits,* I always take the extra precautions, but not with this dog."

The dog continued to stand at attention next to Cindy.

"Did anyone call in about a missing dog?" she asked.

"No mam, not matching his description anyway. I was sure within a few hours someone would be looking for the big guy. He had a blue bandana around his neck, but with no name tag."

His eyes squinted looking worried.

"He was well fed and obviously cared for, but we haven't heard a peep from his owners. If you don't take him, I'm worried he's a goner," the shelter worker said.

"These breeds are difficult to rehome, with a bad reputation. I already got me four *pits* I adopted! Usually I'm able to put down Lab/mix as the breed on the adoption card. It helps get these Pitbulls adopted out, but this guy is such a standout giant..." The man motioned like a mime, with his hands three feet apart, representing the massive size of the dog's square head. "He's the epitome of the American Blue Nose Pitbull, with his cropped ears...I just don't see adoption happening."

"What is this scratch on his hind leg?" Cindy asked the man.

"He had it when we picked him up."

"I'll be honest," Cindy responded. "I don't usually deal with Pitbull's from shelters because I don't know what the previous owners were like, or what bad habits the dog might have picked up."

She reached down, rubbing her hand along the dog's smooth back.

"Just like with any dog from the shelter...you just don't know," she paused for affect. "However, this dog will be training to be a service dog. I need to know it has the correct disposition for this position. How would you feel if I took him for a week in order to assess if he would be a candidate for the program?"

The shelter worker agreed to the return conditions, but Cindy already knew the dog was a keeper.

Leaving the shelter that hot New Mexico afternoon, she

rolled down the windows to release the heat and the wet dog smell from the sealed car. The massive silver dog leaned its head out the window, catching the wind in his lips, letting the insides of his freckled pink flaps vibrate in the breeze.

"You're a handsome boy," she told him with a soothing voice.

After Buster and Cindy returned to *Doggy Stiles Training Center,* she had been able to evaluate him further. Lenny offered him chicken treats from several feet away, trying to entice the dog to disobey. The dog didn't budge. They increased the distractions; Lenny used bikes, rollerblades, he threw balls to the other dogs, while inviting Buster to join. The dog didn't budge. Always keeping its focus on Cindy.

It hadn't been all work and no play. Given the opportunity, Buster was thrilled to romp with Cindy's family dogs, and the service program dogs' Fred and Songbird. He loved the little wieners, and wrestled gently with his big furry pals, gnawing at one another playfully.

One week after Lenny's death, Tamara, watched the silver dog leaping higher than her head each time he retrieved the bright pink Frisbee disk she had tossed. He became a darkening twister in the air, the dog's muscles shuttering with excitement. Tamara had insisted on retaining the one assignment she took seriously at the center.

"It is time for me to name the new dog."

The large *pit* had helped pull Cindy from her funk after Lenny's terrible fall; her energy was spent on training the service animals, instead of crying over Lenny. Her wife had become distraught after finding his soaked body in the front lobby. Tamara had watched Cindy's hands turn pink and raw from the bleach she used to clean the sudsy mess from the porous concrete floor—after the police had cleared the area—ruling it an accidental death. Cindy had worried the rescue dogs would become distressed by the smell of the dog trainer's blood, after all the animals had been through.

"He is an extraordinary athlete," Tamara simpered. "No doubt about it he's mightier than most mutts."

She tossed the Frisbee further than the previous throws. The massive dog caught it, but upon returning it stopped mid-run to gaze intently at Tamara with his gleaming golden eyes.

"That's it!" Tamara jumped up from her cross-legged position on the grass, "I Tamara, best doggone wife ever—designated dog namer to my darling Cindy, the dog tamer—proclaim this indomitable dog to be known as *Buster the Extraordinaire!*"

Tamara was a self-proclaimed "word hound," and as she watched Buster's stormy gray body twisting in the air, she couldn't help but think he looked every bit the second definition of the word—a sudden violent wind coming from the south.

Cindy's own mother had died of Type-two diabetes. She had watched both her mother's feet be amputated. Cindy decided to devote her life, to not only her dog training passion, but also to focus her efforts on fulfilling her life's purpose: to provide people with service dogs to help combat their debilitating disease.

It costs a person upwards of thirty-five thousand dollars

to acquire a service dog through NIDAD, the Institute for Diabetic Alert Dogs. She was able to train and place service dogs at a fraction of the price. Tamara thought Cindy should charge at least twenty thousand dollars per service animal, but Cindy felt she could go as low as ten thousand to help an individual without the financial means to purchase a NIDAD dog.

Several weeks prior to placing Buster with his forever home, Cindy sat in her living room with Clyde on her lap and Bonnie at her feet; she was working on the dog business's budget and checking emails on her laptop, when she opened an email from June Swartz's nephew. The email perfectly coincided with the completion of Buster's service dog requirements:

Dear Ms. Cindy Stiles,

I have been doing quite a bit of research lately on diabetic alert dogs. Most are completely out of our price range. I found you by accident. You see, we need a dog for my Aunt June. She is terribly ill, suffering with confusion, shakiness, and heart palpitations. The hypoglycemic episodes are coming more often. She has a limited budget and is unable to afford assistance. Please let me know if you have a dog available for my aunt. We have started a www.gofundme.com to help with the cost. We are already at $4,300. Let me know what I can do to help with this process.

Kind regards,
  Kyle Swartz

. . .

"Things always work out this way," Cindy gushed. "You send a message out to the universe and *bam* you get an email from Mr. Swartz."

"This is destiny," she yelled to Tamara, who was stretching in the other room.

"You manifested it, Cindy," Tamara said.

This is what Cindy lived for—she only wished Lenny could have seen how Buster turned out.

MY HEART IS ON FIRE. My hind legs burn, the muscles pulling and contracting with each jolting step, as I chase after the dark car. I am angry and sad thinking of him. Running faster. I must catch the car. Lunging at the vehicle, my front paws latch onto the steel trunk. I'm slipping. I fail to hold on, sliding from the back end. Cringing at the screeching sound of my nails slipping against the hot metal. Blazing the purple paint with my mark. I crash onto the burning asphalt, rolling several times. Listening to the rumble of the engine speeding off. Crying out in pain from the fall and from a broken heart.

The sound of my own howling yanks me from my sleep like the jolt at the end of a leash.

I could hear the front doors of the building opening. It was Cindy and her entourage. I listened to the clicking of sixteen paws tap dancing through the lobby.

Breath in. Standing from my spongy mattress to stretch my white paws straight in front of me, with my back end rising like the sun, in proper yoga form. Breath out. Cindy's wife, Tamara, told me people call this morning stretch the *Downward Dog*. I love new words.

I loved Cindy. She smelled like cheese and bacon bits. I think bacon bits might be my favorite food. She handed treats out faithfully as reward for following her commands.

The energy came off her in pulsating amber waves.

"I need to connect with the dog I'm training," she had explained.

We were connected through the cheese...and the bacon bits. I loved her.

After Lenny died, she tried to hold her emotions together for the dogs. We detected Cindy's underlying sadness and the anxiety caused over the loss of her friend, so we tried even harder to be good canine students.

I knew this day was going to be different by the way Cindy approached my kennel. Sensing she was nervous and excited. Mostly, I was thrilled to be getting a piece of cheese, affection, and stimulus. Plus, I was desperate to take a piss. I could hear her boots clonk against the floor, and then the *clink* and the whine of the chain link gate opening. She wheezed through her open mouth from her heaviness. I stood quietly, listening for the rap of her heartbeat; the tick tock of time against her chest. Deep inhale. Sniffing her glucose levels. High. Not high enough to warn her. She smiled down at me, waiting patiently in my kennel.

"Buenos días Señor Buster!"

It didn't matter what language she spoke. It was more important for humans to use the universal language of gestures. Which made it perfect that Cindy trained dogs mainly using sign language commands.

I greeted her in return with the enthusiasm she deserved. She let me smell Luke, Zeek, and the wieners on her pant legs and up her arms. I kissed her face with my not-so-mean mug. Gentle velvet kisses with one small lick. She had just eaten a sausage omelet. She motioned her hand against her thigh for me to follow her down the concrete corridor, out the back door, and onto the agility course arena.

Oh boy! I danced my white paws in front of me, declaring my elation.

We were getting ready to have some fun. She gestured for me to *Sit*.

"Buster today you are going to meet someone special," she sang with excitement.

I had no idea how to read her intonation. I waited.

I could hear movements and voices coming from the building. The back door opened, and two people emerged, following closely behind Cindy's wife. Tamara was always helping at the training center nowadays, since Lenny died.

I watched an elderly woman limping slowly towards me, with her large swollen legs exposed; I could see the pink flesh hanging over the tops of her mid-calf white socks. She was wearing adjustable-strap sandals to fit around her fat feet. She smelled old: of mothballs, urine, Listerine mouthwash, and White Shoulders perfume. Her fuzzy white hair formed a feathery crown. A middle-aged man, wearing wrinkled khaki pants and a collared dark shirt, held the woman's elbow. His round wire-framed glasses pinched the top of his sharp nose.

"Please come and join Buster and me," Cindy invited the couple over.

They were taking particularly cautious miniature steps aimed at the fold-out metal chairs that Tamara had placed next to the agility course, under my favorite tree. The elderly woman shakily lowered herself onto one of them.

"Buster, I want you to meet Aunt June."

"Reach your hand out for Buster to smell," Cindy instructed Aunt June.

I sniffed at her spotted, wrinkled hand, pleased with the odors I encountered: the strong soap and perfume had covered the yummy smell of tuna fish, cookies, prunes, a cat, cat poop in a litter box (a.k.a. Almond Roca), and stagnant dust.

"And Buster this is her nephew Kyle," she said as the stranger reached his hand out for me to smell.

He had that new car smell. Kyle smelled of plastic and Kellogg's Fruit Loops cereal. Fruit Loops had a similar smell to a person with high glucose levels.

"This is a massive dog," Kyle said hesitantly. "How will my elderly aunt be able to keep control of him? I was thinking it would be a golden retriever...or something smaller like a beagle."

"He is but a gentle giant." Cindy smiled brightly. "Buster has never exhibited even the slightest bit of aggression. Honestly, he is one of the most agreeable, well-mannered, intelligent dogs I've come across in my thirty years of dog service. Mark my words, you will never encounter a problem with Buster."

"Can he travel on airplanes?" Kyle asked Cindy. "I have a trip planned next month, to fly Aunt June to Miami to see my mother...her sister."

"Of course!" Cindy exclaimed. "He will have no problem traveling in an airplane. Plus, airlines are extremely accommodating with service dogs."

"How is he around children?" Artificially sweet-smelling Kyle interrogated Cindy.

My white paws began to tap dance at the prospect of being around kids.

"Buster was introduced to the entire Sand Cliffs Preschool. He let the kids crawl all over him, with their sticky fingers fondling his mouth and ears."

"When I introduced him to a cat," she started laughing. Then, recreating the scene, she crouched her knees and splayed her arms out in front of her body. "He carefully dropped to the floor with his two white paws in front of him like an Egyptian Sphinx, then he waited for the cat to come and rub against him, before licking the cat's face clean."

"I don't have kids, but there are lots of little's living in the trailer park," Aunt June giggled. "I do have an old feline friend, Mr. Magoo."

"First, Aunt June needs to set the entire week aside for training intensives and time for bonding with Buster and to gain a better understanding of the proper hand signals," Cindy explained to Kyle, dismissing Aunt June as though she were a child.

Getting to know Aunt June was easy. She was fragile although hefty. Aunt June had lost everyone she knew, that is what she told me, all but her nephew Kyle. Divulging that all her family and friends had either "passed on" or were "barely living" in nursing homes.

"My husband Wilber died after having a stroke ten years ago, when he was seventy-eight years old," she told me, sitting on the folding chair, under the tree, next to the agility course. "It was a good life for him... and he was happy when he passed on."

I wasn't sure what "passed on" meant, but I associated it with the "final walk" the downtrodden dogs took at the shelter.

I liked how she talked to me like I was her friend. I was.

She lost her son Ralph in a jet boating accident. Her twin sister had died slipping down the tiled concrete stairs leading into a pool, hitting her head against the ledge—kind of like Lenny—I remembered his blood blending with the sudsy water.

"I guess it was a real mess," she told me.

Her and Wilber had spent their entire lives managing a bowling alley they didn't own in Forked River, New Jersey. Upon the sale of the alley, with no retirement to speak of, except for a small social security stipend, the couple decided it was time for some warmth and relaxation. They chose to retire to the Cottonwood Estates Trailer Park, ideally located just outside Albuquerque. The trailer park came with all the amenities: a pool and Jacuzzi, shuffle-board, and a putting green. Behind her trailer was an endless expanse of yellow desert and tumbleweeds. This is where Aunt June continued to reside.

"The property was affordable and the weather hot," she told me, dabbing sweat from her brow with a tissue.

I was happy to love Aunt June and planned to take good care of her.

I was aware of the tingly sweet scent associated with an impending diabetic emergency. The smells made me want to sneeze; instead I would go *tze tze* between my teeth—saliva spritzing those around me—I was taught to paw at Aunt June's leg.

"It's the change in a person's scent from having high blood sugar levels," Cindy had explained during training.

―――――――――

"There will be five separate test sites we'll be using," Cindy interrupted my thoughts. "We will be following the standards of the ODOR Service Dogs Inc," she droned on. "We will be testing his alertness in numerous situations; noisy distraction and anywhere that is unfamiliar to the dog."

We started the test sites by visiting Aunt June's trailer park. Walking through the rows of single-wide trailers, I was bombarded by a multitude of distractions; each modular home emitted its own distinct odor, the sound of dogs yipping and howling from open windows and fenced yards, food distractions from the dumpsters at the end of the park, and strangers calling out to me. Fire hydrants. I ignored it all.

I watched Aunt June wobble out onto the rickety wooden porch of her avocado green, single-wide trailer. She was smiling joyfully at our arrival. This made me happy. My non-existent nub-of-a-tail wagged with delight. The old wooden porch planks creaked under the strain of our mutual weight as Cindy and I joined Aunt June on the front patio.

Walking into the house I was swamped by the sensory overload.

"Aunt June is a hoarder," Cindy later explained to me when we returned to the shelter. I assumed that meant she liked stuff; *hoarder* was a new word.

Inside the dark paneled trailer, we found furniture piled high, coffee tables, and side tables were stacked on top of one another, each corner, crevice and shelf jammed with crafty items.

"I love to sew and craft, as you can see," Aunt June told Cindy. "I've also purchased some items from the church craft bazaar and Saturday morning yard sales."

I sniffed at a chalk-covered painted ceramic sign, engraved with the unfamiliar words: *Smile, God loves you.*

Moving on to the little dust-bunny dolls in home knitted outfits, sitting next to needlework pillows inscribed with phrases: *The Smallest Things Bring the Greatest Joy...Follow your Dreams...Thankful Grateful Blessed*. She had filthy orange, red and yellow hexagonal-patterned afghan blankets smelling forty years old, with matching knitted armrest covers on her chairs and couch. I knew her chair was the cream colored one with the urine stains. The smell hit me like a fifty-pound bag of dog food. I wanted to lift my leg and cover the chair with my own scent, but I knew better, and respected her territory. Sniffing around the boxes filled with old mothball covered clothing; I began exploring down the hallway with my nose, finding my way into the back bedroom.

Three human heads waited for me on a dresser along the paneled wall to my right. They stopped me in my tracks, prompting me with an urgent desire to backpedal my way out of the room, but Aunt June stood behind me blocking my hasty departure. She must be a psychopath! Each head had the same short gray blond hair and no eyes or mouths. They smelled of Aunt June and Styrofoam. I might have overreacted.

"Silly pup, are you scared of my mannequins?" Aunt June asked me giggling. "They're made to hold my wigs. I don't bother with them wigs much anymore. No need to play dress up with Wilber gone."

She had dresses hanging from wheeled clothing racks lining the walls. An unused ironing board was piled high with discarded dresses and shirts, propped in the middle of the room; the iron cord swirling to the floor. A vanity had accumulated unopened cosmetic boxes and bottles of perfume. The wall behind it was covered in costume jewelry that hung from hooks drilled in diamond patterns.

Boxes lay open with fancy fake gold and silver bracelets and sparkling jeweled earrings spilling out. The carpet was old. I smelled layers of dirt, years of faded odors, emitting the slight whiff of a dog long ago. Leaving the room with the head trickery, I smelled the sweetness of old man Wilber's aftershave seeping from the bathroom.

I think Aunt June was lonelier than me when I was sat abandoned in the cold shelter cell. I smelled her seclusion biting at the air, as my nose led me back towards the living room, sniffing the carpet edges deeply. One large inhale made me halt—one white paw paused mid-step.

"A cat!"

My nose was drawn to the one-inch crack under the closed panel door on my right. I inhaled as if it was my first breath on earth. Aunt June had a cat. I wanted to append myself to him.

"Buster, do you want to be introduced to Mr. Magoo?" Cindy asked.

I lay down with my white paws pointing towards the closed door. My bum wiggled. They had started saying "Buster" in front of most sentences when addressing me. I understood it to be my new name. It was branded on the shiny red biscuit tag hanging from my new collar, decorated in green Saguaro cacti.

"Buster, I guess that's a yes!" Cindy was laughing at my eagerness.

Aunt June opened the door and a crippled scraggly white cat emerged from the darkened room. The cat was missing most of his teeth, with one extra-long fang forming a snaggletooth over his lower paper-thin lip. He smelled like cat litter. Hissing all the while, as he strutted towards me. I didn't flinch, but my eyes began blinking rapidly—the whites exposed.

Please don't scratch out my eyeballs, I tried to send him the message telepathically.

The cat came closer hissing a little softer. I could feel his fur gently caress my spikey whiskers. Then the pussy rubbed its cotton soft body hard against my neck and face.

Oh, for the love of sweet Jesus!

I had all but died and gone to heaven.

It wouldn't be a bad gig I told myself. I liked the stories the smells from her manufactured home told. The home provided a dark cave-like ambiance—the drapes closed it was déjà vu—the familiarity was right.

I would be trading one good life for another.

"Being a service dog is a very fulfilling lifestyle," Cindy chatted at Aunt June. "Are you looking forward to your trip to Miami?"

"Oh yes, very much so...I think Buster is going to love the beach...but wait...does he know how to swim?"

AS HAPPY AS A DOG WITH TWO TAILS

CARMEN WAS A STRONG, intelligent Cuban American woman. Nobody seemed to notice. Her beauty blinded people.

It was happening once again with the perverted TSA Officer, Randy.

"Put your hands above your head and turn around," the paunchy uniformed man demanded, twisting his porn 'stache into a creepy smirk.

He licked his open wet lips, leaving behind a residue of saliva on the 'stache's bristles. His eyes began stripping off her flight attendant uniform, unbuttoning her blouse one snap at a time. No laws against imagination. She was regularly forced to abide by Randy's requests on the routine Las Vegas layover. Ordinarily, she made it a point to arrive at the airport with the rest of the flight crew, so she could slip past the lewd official. But today she had called her parents in Miami; the phone call had run long, forcing her to take a later hotel airport shuttle than her co-workers.

Carmen was on the last leg of her last flight, completing a three-day shift, finally returning home to Miami.

Her night in Vegas was ordinary and uncomplicated; how she liked it. After using the hotel gym, she had a yogurt berry parfait from room service before inserting her earplugs and falling deep asleep.

When in Miami, she liked to kick box at the gym around the corner from her South Beach apartment. Returning home to relax with her white longhaired Persian cat, Feliz, his soft vibrating purr would fill Carmen's lap and heart with happiness. She was fine to crunch carrot sticks and sip cheap chardonnay in the full blast of the air-conditioner, with only the cat for company, be it swinging his white tail in her warm bath water or getting frisky chasing the catnip filled toy mice around the apartment. She needed him like the cat kneaded Carmen's smooth tan legs with its sharp claws, flicking its tail gently under her nose to leave microscopic hairs for her to sneeze out.

It would seem Carmen's beauty was a first-class golden ticket to an easier life. She would always get the job and the guy. After being pulled over more than a dozen times she had never received a speeding ticket. However, showing its ugly face to her outward grace, was that she trusted only a few people to see past this gifted attractiveness—to see her—and that was her family.

This morning's phone call to her family was about Papi's upcoming retirement party. He was leaving the Miami boat marina he had been an outboard engine mechanic at for over thirty years. Her mother, Luz, would continue volunteering at the multi-cultural center, with her focus being full time *abuela* to Carmen's three brother's growing families.

On the weekends they would get together for large family dinners. Carmen and Papi would dance around the house, taking turns playing the accordion. Her brothers had shown zero interest in learning their father's musical passion. Papi and Carmen made quite a team, even performing for neighborhood *fiestas*, shaking their hips and dancing with the full band; a mother-of-pearl accordion strapped to each of their chests.

Carmen now appeared in stark contrast to her former brace-faced child self, who had flaunted a bowl-shaped haircut, her mother's attempt at saving money by making the kitchen into a makeshift beauty salon.

She had learned to keep up with the two older brothers, while her younger brother birddogged after her. The four kids would spend their summers at the boat marina. Boats lined the marina's walls from floor to ceiling. They were told to keep out of the way, so they took to hiding behind the mangroves by the old lobster trap piles—passing time building forts, playing cards, wrestling for bets, and slinging rocks at targets. To make her feel special, being the only girl, her Papi would throw down a large piece of cardboard over the oil-slicked floor of his shop, providing her a place to play with her Barbie dolls. Sometimes he would flip over a bucket, so she could color or work on her school studies.

"Carmen, your nose is running," he used to lovingly take the front of his greasy work shirt and hold it to her face. "Blow hard."

Her Papi would give the siblings equal turns taking test rides on the new twenty-four-foot center console fishing boats, with dual outboard engines. The Aqua Sports and Sea Crafts were cleverly named, with flashy stencil writing on the sides or backends: *Liquor Snapper, Playin Hookie,* or *Chasin Tail*.

When she went with her dad on these test drives, he would max out the speed, her brown hair whipping in wind, becoming caught in her braced smile. She learned to use her sea legs, rebounding with each bump on her scrawny limbs, as the boat banged against the cresting waves.

He would type in the location coordinates on the GPS to his favorite fishing holes. The cell phone-sized machine beeping, as the sonar bounced back from the coral reef sea bottom, forming fluorescent green jagged lines on the screen. When they would arrive at the fishing hole, Papi would pull off his oil stained blue work shirt, with his name, Luis Fuentes, embroidered on the chest. The shirt off revealed his darkly tanned arms, face, and neck, nearly black from the sun, contrasted against his white chest, several small dark hairs popping out above his heart. He would dip his mask and snorkel in the ocean water, spitting and rubbing the saliva over the glass with his thin fingers to keep the mask from fogging. Slipping his feet into the flippers, he would place the mask over his head, chewing down on the snorkel bite. As he sat on the edge of the boat, he would hold his spear gun high above his head, flipping backwards into the ocean water. But, not before yelling into his snorkel a muffled, "Bombs away!"

Papi emerged within a minute or two for a breath of air, or to hold up a freshly speared Brown Spotted Grouper or a Red Snapper. Sometimes he carried the tickle stick for tickling the lobster antennae; teasing the crustacean to back into the waiting mesh bag he held behind its tail. Then he would clip the bounty to his work shorts and swim to the surface for a breath of air. Her mother Luz would make the whole fish, frying it Cuban style; served with black beans, yellow rice and fried plantains.

It might have been her Cuban DNA that caused her to be so fiercely independent. Her parents frowned on Cuban politics and disagreed with Cuba giving women equal constitutional rights as men.

"You guys prefer America's system of giving women seventy percent pay and scant political representation," she complained to her brothers around the backyard patio table after Sunday dinner.

They smiled dismissively at her feminist remarks.

Cuban women average three divorces—Carmen never married. Women are often highly educated doctors and lawyers, climbing to success, thanks to Cuba's family planning program offering free birth control. Carmen was climbing to success using her own means for birth control—simply declining men—like Cuba's declining birth rate.

Carmen had all but given up on a lover. No man could live up to her own high standards. She held this impossible male archetype well into her early thirties. After several therapy sessions she came to realize her benchmark was impossible to meet, because her Papi, Luis Fuentes was perfect. He was kind, humorous, devoted and present. Nobody could compare.

She wheeled the hard-shelled carry-on luggage behind her as she stiffly approached the gate for Flight 982. Her hair was blown out in thick dark waves over her buttoned navy jacket. It was time to put the reclusive introverted face away. It was time to perform for an audience of passengers. Her glossed lips beamed radiantly as she approached the airline staff gathered near the entrance to the airplane corridor. She was thrilled to see her co-worker and devilishly handsome friend, Nicco, standing with the group. His fresh face smiled back at her. He was looking spiffy in his tidy navy uniform. She hadn't realized he would be working the flight to Miami with her.

With her attention focused on Nicco, she clumsily stumbled over a massive silver dog. The wheels of the suitcase brushed over the tops of his white-tipped paws.

Carmen's brilliant smile dropped with concern for the poor pup. The dog had barely flinched and instead lifting its chunky lips into a monstrous grin.

"I'm sorry buddy," she said smiling apologetically to its owner.

The dog raised its eyebrows twitching them back and forth as he looked at Carmen and then back to his owner.

"His name is Buster," the dog's person, a frizzy haired old woman creaked. "Don't worry...he's the friendliest dog in the world."

THE BOARDING CALL for passengers traveling with young children resonated through the airport for Freedom Airlines Flight 982, Las Vegas to Miami, bringing Betsy temporarily out of the baby coma she had been living in for the last three years from sleep deprivation. The baby must be sucking the brain cells out of her; cutest vampire she ever saw. It was a difficult trip for a single mother, a three-year-old, and a newborn baby.

She sat cross-legged on the hard, dark-gray Berber style carpet, under the floor-to-ceiling windows facing the runway. She chose the location, because it was out of the way from the human bustle of the concourse. A spot less trafficked; a space that would keep Blake entertained watching the airplanes take off and land. He had six match-box-sized planes lined up in a row. Reaching out for one with his small chubby hand, dimples dotted above each finger, he squeezed the plane and shot it forward into the air.

"Vroom...swish," he made take off sounds, the spittle flying out his little mouth from between his gapped teeth.

He looked like Betsy. They both had straight brown hair; hers was long in a braid to the side, and his was buzzed short in a military cut. Both their faces were sprinkled with freckles, huge blue eyes, and thick black eyelashes.

"Blake it's time you help mama and sister board the new plane," Betsy explained wearily to her son. They were halfway through their cross-country journey from Anchorage, Alaska to Miami, Florida.

"The two US cities couldn't be further apart," she had told her mother after booking the flight. "We're leaving the darkest state to fly to the sunniest state."

When they landed in Las Vegas after the six-hour red-eye flight from Anchorage, she tried to wake Blake who was dead asleep in his seat, but the more she coddled him the more he refused to open his thick lashed eyes, hunkering deeper into his comfortable window seat. She recognized her predicament while holding the huge diaper bag full of coloring books, toys, electronics, diapers, wipes, several changes of clothes, fresh baked oatmeal cookies, raisins and Goldfish snacks. In addition, she carried an oversized purse with the travel itinerary, computer, a clean shirt, toothbrush and her iPhone.

Her face must have registered the panic she felt.

"Can I help you carry the boy off the plane," a kind stranger asked.

She reluctantly agreed. The man followed behind her ferrying Blake in his arms, down the concourse to Gate 14, placing the semi-awake toddler on a chair in the same space that the little family continued to hold hostage for the duration of three-hour layover. Blake set up his command center near the window, with an expansive view of the air traffic control tower. He leaned his head back to look up at her with the toy plane in mid-air take off.

"We go up, mama!"

"Yes baby, we are going up, this will be our last flight before grandma and grandpa pick us up at the airport in Miami. I bet you can't wait to see your grandparents...right honey?" She spoke to him with sweet exhaustion. "Please clean up your planes and put them into your new big boy backpack."

His chubby fingers started collecting the planes, and one by one he zoomed them into the pack. He uncurled his crossed legs and stood a couple feet tall. Betsy checked Clarabelle's diaper; thankfully it was dry and clean. She placed the baby gently into the Maya wrap, wrapping her close to her own body. The indigenous wrap provided privacy for breastfeeding and freed her hands in case she needed to chase Blake. Betsy gathered the remaining belongings, holding the boarding tickets in her hand.

"Ready Freddie?" She asked her sweet boy, as he stomped in quick circles watching his red Converse shoes gain speed.

He stumbled with the backpack breaking his fall.

"Mama, who wis Freddie?"

He pointed to a plane outside the window that was taxiing onto the runway.

"Is that our pwane?"

"No honey, that plane already has its people on it, and is getting ready to take off, we are going on that one right there," she pointed to the correct plane.

Life seemed heavy at the moment. The weight of her own body weighed down by travel bags, the twelve-pound baby in her arms, and a heavy heart from knowing her husband cheated on her with the waitress at the Clam Shell Lodge. It seemed like too much to bear. With no choice she carried the load like she carried her post baby weight. She was wearing mom jeans and a baggy maroon breastfeeding shirt, with hidden flaps; making her engorged breasts easily accessible to feed the baby. It was also loose around the midsection to help hide her extended tummy.

Betsy had eaten half a pot brownie after landing in Las Vegas and was feeling more relaxed and less anxious traveling with the children. She looked adoringly at Clarabelle's baby doll face sleeping soundly, the delicate porcelain perfection wrapped snugly against her warm body. The baby's cheeks painted rosy and pink; the little girl was not the least bit bothered by the jarring movements Betsy made collecting their belongings.

People in first class had already lined up to board the flight. Her family of three had been invited to skip to the front of the regular economy line to pre-board. The attendant had called for those traveling with small children, she thought defensively, feeling the stares from other passengers, probably hoping her little family wasn't sitting next to them.

Blake spotted a massive Pitbull garbed in a red vest and began to approach the animal. The dog intently stared back at her small boy.

"No, Blake. Don't touch that dog," she called to him.

He turned back to her with his brows furrowed, questioning her reasoning.

Betsy put her hand on her son's shoulder and turned his body to face the ticket agent, giving him a directive shove.

She took a long look at the giant dog calmly waiting its turn to board. Then she looked at Blake who had just stopped, dropped, and rolled in the middle of the boarding line for no apparent reason. People would rather sit next to a well-behaved dog than a kid any day.

Betsy's dog should have been on the flight. She had

booked him a ticket for one-hundred-dollars to ride locked in a crate with the luggage in the airplane's cargo hold. He was the friendliest dog ever and she had thought about getting him an emotional support dog certificate, so he could ride in the cabin with her instead of the dark rumbling guts of the airplane.

"That dog is a service animal, Blake. We aren't supposed to pet the working dogs," She explained as she struggled to assist the child to stand and continue walking to the gate agent.

The frowning uniformed attendant, with a thickly hair sprayed blond bouffant, addressed her son, "What is your name?"

"Bwake Wuv," he confidently responded, as he put his hands behind the straps of his new blue Super Wing's backpack, leaning back on his heels.

The agent handed back the paper tickets with the seat assignment printed on them.

"Have a nice flight," she said in a monotone, before looking up to the muscular redheaded passenger next in line.

Blake ran ahead. Betsy carried Clarabelle and the bags, trudging after him down the long gray-carpeted corridor bay. The flight crew greeted them at the entrance to the airplane. Then the young family crept down the aisle, waiting for the first-class passengers to finish putting away their luggage in the overhead compartments and to position themselves comfortably into their oversized chairs. One handsome, well-dressed man appeared to have already been served a cocktail. He took a sip and leaned the seat back. He was built strong like her husband Jared, with his same dark eyes and hair, but the crisp new Patagonia clothing the man had on wasn't anything like the oil stained Carhartts and holey Helly Hansen sweatshirt Jered favored. The family proceeded past first-class, through the separation wall, to view the empty rows of economy class stretched in front of them.

"Keep going Blake, look for row 10E and F," she said this knowing he would have no idea where that was.

"Dis pwane is smaw!" Blake walking ahead shouted back at her in a shrill voice.

This was the smaller body Boeing 737; he was comparing it to the wide body, two-aisle wide Airbus they flew down from Anchorage.

"Stop, Blake," she commanded the boy, "That's our row."

Taking the load off her tender shoulders, she dropped the bags onto the aisle seat, and then proceeded to remove Clarabelle from the wrap.

"Only one more leg of the trip to go," she sighed. "The worst is over."

———

Betsy started her home bakery business several years before having Blake. She had planned on purchasing a brick-and-mortar store with the profits, but babies change plans. All the meticulously designed, sweet, sugary, edible art was done under a swinging full-spectrum light bulb hanging above her kitchen island. Feeding her freckled, translucent skin the vitamin D she lacked from the northern winter exposure.

She didn't allow the long Alaskan winters to bring her down into the darkness of depression like it did so many others. For optimal sunshine exposure, she was sure to spend the afternoons outside when the sun was at its highest point in the sky, hovering on the horizon. The sky would turn purple, pink and orange, reflecting off the frozen hoarfrost that covered the earth to create a picture beyond her imagination: a shimmering tree-lined, crystalized winter wonderland.

She had rigged a child's plastic sled to a harness strapped around her waist, so the kids could join her on snow-filled adventures. She would click into her cross-country skis, pulling Blake in the long red sled, as she carried Clarabelle strapped snug against her chest. Betsy would follow the snow machine and dog musher tracks. Going for miles along the tree-lined, snow-packed trails, before either kid would become antsy. Her rule was to never go skiing when the temperatures dipped below eight degrees.

The Service Dog they had just passed as they entered the corridor to the plane compelled Betsy to think about her Australian Shepherd mix, Salty Dog, and how he flaunted a frosty beard made of icicle whiskers on the winter rides. Bounding ahead, his gray and white fur coat disappearing completely under the deep snow, with an explosion of white when he would break free from the frozen snow crust. The vast loneliness of the land came to life with the dog's snowy gait. He had a cheerful disposition and complete relish for life. He was thrilled every time she pulled out her ski boots from the mudroom. For that matter, he would show spirited zeal each time she stood from her creaky worn recliner after feeding Clarabelle or went outside to chop wood for the stove. A full dish of food would reveal his appetite for life, as would a new thrift store plush toy, or discovering an abandoned carcass half eaten by the wolves and scavenger eagles—a fresh juicy knuckle—bone harmony.

Salty's wagging appendage was bedeviled by two-foot length strands of fur that knocked every full glass of wine, juice and milk off the coffee table. Stains covered the living room carpet from his wagging eagerness. His shaggy tail would swish past Betsy's cacti plants, collecting a spiked succulent to form a swinging barbed medieval flail. Detailed thousand-piece puzzles were a thing of the past, between Blake's grabby fingers, and Salty Dog's furry tail madness.

The dog's fate became a Disney's *Lady and the Tramp* scenario. Salty Dog took a backseat after two babies were born within a several years of one another. Literally, he rode in the back of the pickup truck.

"Get off the couch Salty!" Her husband Jared shouted, showing his irritation by scrunching his dark eyebrows together.

"He isn't hurting anyone," Betsy would defend the dog.

Jared would hold his angry glare, while raising his voice, and changing his irritable focus to the messy house.

"Look at the hair on the couch," he would pinch a clump of white fur between his fingers, holding it up for her to view. "It's everywhere. That dog could jump on the baby. Keep him off the couch. You need to vacuum the house. Disgusting. Fur is going to end up in your cakes and you'll get sued."

Salty Dog was fed a grain-free diet, one and a half cups twice a day, so he didn't itch from his wheat allergy. The sound of the dog tags clanking and tinkling together when the dog itched drove Jared mad.

Jared worked two weeks on shift on an oilrig in the icy waters of the Cook Inlet, Alaska—rotating two weeks at home. When he was home, he mostly played with his friends; fishing for salmon and halibut all summer, hunting for moose and bear in the fall, heading to the Caribou Hills to ride snow machines during the winter. It was probably best he went away to do his drinking. Best he was not around the kids, as far as she was concerned. Betsy led a lonely, busy life.

The same week she had decided to leave Alaska—to leave Jared—Salty Dog joined Betsy and the kids for his final ski. The dog bounded ahead. She noticed he had spotted something off the trail and went to investigate. Betsy's skis came to a sliding stop; the sound of the friction on the squeaky snow and her heavy breathing quieted. Silence. No birds. No motors. Even the shimmering snow falling from a branch was dampened. She saw movement to her right and caught a glimpse of his gray fur bobbing in the deep snow.

Slam!

It was the sound of an animal traps icy metal jaws clamping shut. Followed by sound of her dog's silent struggle howling through the winter wonderland.

Betsy had Clarabelle strapped to her chest. Blake was sitting in the sled. Her breath quickened as she unhooked the harness strap around her waist, with her quivering, fleece-gloved hands. She stepped her skis off the musher track into the four-foot-deep white powder, sinking down into the snow she held her daughter's head with one hand, struggling to move deeper.

Betsy could see Salty grappling against the trap ten feet away. She gradually started breaking a trail towards her trapped friend. The dog had started to slow his struggle by the time she arrived. One agonizing minute felt multiplied by ten. It was his last minute; during which he flipped and flopped and twisted in harrowing pain. She reached down to investigate the conibear traps claws, gruesomely digging its spiked jaws into Salty's neck and head. Clarabelle's neck noodled, jouncing against the baby carrier, as Betsy struggled to free the dog.

"Salty, I'm here baby," she could feel warm salty tears freezing to her face.

She tried to pull the bloodied trap apart with her gloved hands, but it wouldn't budge. Salty's body stopped moving. He lay still. She petted his warm fur with her gloved hand.

"No, this isn't happening." She whispered into the snow muffled silence.

She kneeled in the frost next to his body, taking her gloves off, she attempted to pry the trap open with her bare hands. Her sunglasses fogged from her labored breathing; the moisture from her tears and the snot dripping from her nose. She threw the steamed glasses into the snow. Betsy looked for a spring release or for any button that might loosen the traps death grip. Clarabelle began to cry from all the rough jarring movements her mom was making.

"Mama, come bac'!" Blake screamed out to her.

She turned to see him through her blurred eyes; he was standing in the red sled looking her way. She started packing the trail down by taking extended strides with her skis towards him, holding Clarabelle tightly to her chest. When she returned to Blake, she took Clarabelle out of the front carrier and laid her flat on her back atop the sled. The baby wore a warm, blue down snowsuit with fur trim lining her doll face; a Blake hand-me-down. Her daughter would be warm enough.

"Blake, Salty Dog has been hurt by an animal trap and he has died," she sniffled, and then asked her three-year-old, "Do you understand?"

"What happen to Swalty?" he asked furrowing his brow with worry, the spitting image of his father.

"I'm going to get him, and you need to be a big boy and

take care of your sister while I'm gone. Can you do that Blake?"

He nodded his small head with astute understanding.

She was much quicker returning to her dead dog, after the snowy path had been packed down, and with no baby in her arms. She pulled the trap from the frozen ground and attempted to lift the lifeless animal. Quickly realizing she couldn't lift his dead weight. She dragged Salty's body, holding him by his hind legs through the snow, making a bloody trail across the white, but he was too heavy. She dropped his body. Panting from the exertion, she retreated to her waiting children, her breath fogging the air.

"Blake, sit in the snow and hold Clarabelle in your lap until I return."

She pulled the red sled over to Salty Dog, lifting and dragging his quickly cooling body onto the plastic toy. His disfigured face had frozen into an anguished snarl. Blood poured from the jagged wounds around his crown and throat. The red ice was freezing to the trap. She was willing to suffer the monetary fine, a consequence of illegally removing the legal trap. She couldn't leave him out in the forest for the wolves to eat.

"Fuck you, trapper!" She screamed, huffing and puffing for momentum to drag the dead dog onto the sled.

Latching the sled to her waist strap, she pulled the dog back to her frightened children. She took off her jacket to cover her friend, hiding the dog's punctured body from her son. Then she lifted Clarabelle from Blake's slight arms and slipped her into the front carrier.

"Blake, hop on the sled with Salty Dog."

GOING TO THE DOGS

"Folks call me Derek Beeman," the statuesque man said with his hand extended, while standing in front of the mirrored back drop of the bar, reflecting his new designer travel apparel.

He spoke with a slight Australian twang when he introduced himself to the middle-aged blonde man wearing an expensive suit. The blond man had a small scar running from the middle of his cheek to the edge of his thin upper lip. Derek recognized the guy; he just hadn't placed him yet.

When Derek entered the airport bar, he immediately homed in on the sharply dressed man. Choosing the stool one over from him, so to admire the man's gold Rolex and three-thousand-dollar designer suit. Chances were high they would both be flying first class to Miami. The well-dressed man returned the handshake firmly.

"Nice to meet you, Mr. Beeman. I'm Florida Senator Mike Young," he motioned to the attractive forty-or-so-year-old woman on his right, introducing her with a friendly drawl, "And this is my lovely assistant, Ms. Stacy Pettington."

Derek had in fact heard of the Florida senator. He considered himself a human name index. Remembering the faces and names of every individual, their wives, children, and even their dogs.

Derek considered himself a seasoned world traveler and an adventure enthusiast. His job often assigned him to the most desirable destinations, and exploitable world locations, to scout out production venues. He had been raised surrounded by the farmlands and vineyards of Adelaide, Australia, and as a young teen, he spent the summers with his father, taking tourists on cage diving shark tours off the south coast. When Derek was fifteen his father had been offered a job opportunity to dive the oil platforms in the Gulf of Mexico, choosing to relocate the family to Houston, Texas.

Derek was senior consultant for Outstanding Trips Abroad Inc.; a company specializing in planning film locations, as well as the implementation of special requirements needed by movie and television production companies from around the world. His last project had been planning an exciting educational episode, allowing TV viewers to follow the fearless, risk-taking Chef Kevin Fontaine, sampling the indigenous delicacies with locals, traveling across Myanmar, with the number one rated food program *Experience Eating*.

With the undertaking, Derek was tasked to organize filmable locations, and plan the travel itinerary by plane, train, and by bus through the volatile country not well traveled by Hollywood. The assignment entrusted Derek with keeping Fontaine in front of the golden-tipped temples, highlighting the star's golden mop and deep dimples. Also, Derek was charged with keeping the food guru and film crews away from the Buddhist Myanmar security forces, driving the Muslim Rohingyas from their land; burning down their mosques, looting and setting fire to their homes, along with raping the women. It didn't make for good Food Network television.

Recently Derek had been consulting on a more local level for a movie currently being filmed in Florida. The directors were looking for white sand beaches, without sunburned tourists peeling about. The task wasn't as hard as he thought it would be. He dismissed searching the devastated beaches of central Florida, covered in a nasty-smelling red alga, stemming from the Lake Okeechobee runoff. Instead, he aimed his attention south towards Miami.

"The secluded "local" beaches are no longer a secret after I pull out this wad of hundred-dollar bills," he would say when bragging about his negotiation skills.

The second request proved more difficult. The directors wanted to film a high-speed boat chase in Miami-Dade County river waters, deemed Manatee Protection Zones by the Fish and Wildlife Conservation Commission. He had spent weeks attempting to bribe county officials to grant a pass, filing numerous requests for one-time use permits.

"The only way to get a speed boat on that river is to get legislation passed allowing motorboats in the manatee protected areas," explained a cranky bureaucrat. "You'll also need to increase the speed limits in those protected areas."

He was told that several key Florida senators had been working on game changing amendments to the current conservation laws; making efforts to end protections in certain Florida waters. One of these senators was Mike Young, sitting next to him shaking his hand.

"Yea mate, think we have time to grab a bite to eat?" Derek asked the senator. "I'm starved, and I sure as shit don't want any airplane food. You're flying to Miami, right?"

Derek tried not to work the guy too hard. Hold back, he reminded himself. *Don't be a space-invader.* He held his award-winning grin waiting for the senator's reply.

"I'm so hungry I could eat a horse," the scar above the senator's lip curled into a crescent moon when he smiled, "and I'm willing to bet the food on the plane will likely taste like dog meat."

Derek hailed the bartender, by saluting his arm, with a small dismissive wave. When the bartender arrived, he ordered a cold one, and eighteen spicy chicken wings, with blue cheese dip.

"Would you like another cocktail, Senator?"

The senator nodded to the bartender signaling for one more.

"Speaking of food tasting like dog," Derek started. "I was scouting out locations in a town in central Vietnam called Ninh Binh. The town is a couple hours south of Hanoi by train. It's well known in Vietnam for its goat delicacies—and spelunking, but that's another story...."

Derek was looking for acknowledgment from the senator. He could see he was losing the man by the way he stirred the speared olive in his martini, focusing his attention on the baseball game playing on the flat screen above the bar.

"Like I said, the town is known for its gourmet goat cuisine," Derek started again raising his voice a notch and speaking slower. "I was scouting out locations for a TV program...you might have heard of Kevin Fontaine?"

The senator stopped stirring his drink and turned his gaze to Derek. His interest was piqued once again.

"I might know of that program."

"Well, you see I was consulting for the studio, so in this case traveling on my own budget, staying in the seedier places...if you will. The hostel was clean enough, but my room was four flights up a steep staircase, and bloody freezing."

Derek chortled as he took a sip of his beer; the froth left a brew mustache reminiscent to the Nazi Adolf Hitler's above his upper lip.

"I asked the front desk attendant where a good place to eat goat meat would be. Getting the local input is always key to really experiencing the culture you are in. The hotel clerk ordered me a taxi, letting the driver know where to go. I was unfamiliar with the town and as the driver turned down side street after side street...yeah, I became disoriented. The taxi pulls into a dead-end alley next to a dark stained concrete restaurant with large windows, shuttered for the winter, with no identifying sign hanging out front. The driver motioned for me to get out. I paid him ten thousand dong and slammed the door, crossing my fingers I would find a taxi back to the hotel after dinner."

"I was then ushered to a seat at an empty table set for eight. A petite woman produced a laminated menu and set a glass of warm water in front of me that I hadn't planned on drinking if I didn't want to bloody shit my pants for the next week. The menu was printed completely in Vietnamese; I turned it over and tried reading the sub-lines. The menu had zero English words and I don't speak but a few words of Vietnamese...so it was useless. Of course, the waitress didn't speak English either. I had obviously accomplished my mission of jumping off the beaten path!"

Derek laughed heartily. The senator was rapt with his story. He had succeeded in gaining the prominent man's attention. The bartender returned with the chicken wings, setting out small plates in front of each of them, napkins and wet wipes for the secretary Stacy, Derek, and the senator.

"At the top of the menu," Derek held his large arms out acting like he was holding a menu and pointed to the top section. "There was a tiny picture of a goat in the corner. I pointed to it and the waitress nodded understanding, then she ran off to put my order in. At that same time, I observed a family, sitting at a table near my own, being served a large portion of steaming stew, accompanied by the perfect fresh baked French baguettes overflowing the basket."

He held his large hands a foot apart to describe the size of the fresh bread.

"The sheila returned with a plate of mixed greens; basil, mint, and other mixed herbs...rice papers for rolling the thinly shaved goat meat and herb mix...along with a delicious light sauce served on the side for dipping."

His dark eyes looked off longingly thinking of the Vietnamese meal, while he licked wing sauce from his juicy lips.

"I just couldn't get that stew out of my mind, and I tried asking the waitress what it was called by pointing to the meal being devoured by the family next to me. The waitress indicated the item on the menu...but it was in Vietnamese. I pointed again to my neighbor's food and requested one for myself, by signaling one with my finger."

Derek raised his thick square pointer finger, aiming it at the ceiling.

"She returned with my stew shortly after and I dipped the warm scrumptious French bread into the thick broth. Potatoes and carrots were mixed with squared beef-like meat. I dug in and ate the warm stew. It wasn't bad; the broth was seasoned nicely. It was the perfect meal for that cold winter night.

I noticed it didn't taste like the goat I had just eaten, and it definitely was not beef; with the fat gristle holding tight to the edges of meat chunks. The texture was different. While I sat contemplating the flavor, I heard barking coming from behind the kitchen. I looked out my window through the wooden slats. Behind me, next to the kitchen I noticed several mutt dogs tied with ropes to metal hooks along a concrete wall. I kept chewing—and then with a sort of realization I opened my napkin and spit the bite out of my mouth."

The senator looked at Derek seemingly confused.

"Why would you spit it out?"

"Because it was dog, man!" Stacy rasped while sucking on a chicken wing.

Derek didn't really have a problem with eating dog per say. It wasn't his favorite meat—with its gristle and gaminess. Most people found the unappetizing story funny and disgusting. The truth was he saw no difference eating one species from another. Forgone conclusions regarding food were based solely on a person's culture. Not taste. He had learned that from food guru Kevin Fontaine.

Derek watched a feather-light blond woman walk into the bar, dressed in periwinkle pants and matching shirt. She glided on her toes like a ballerina dancer, before requesting a glass of chardonnay.

"They told me the black dogs taste the best...ha ha ha," Derek chortled, "but I'll tell you one thing brother...dog doesn't taste like chicken!"

The senator stretched his arm out to inspect his Rolex.

"Looks like it's just about time to board our flight and I could sure use another drink."

She had never received so much attention as today. It wasn't her on the receiving end really, it was Buster who was getting all the complements and straight up gawking by strangers. She knew he was an impressive animal to look at with his substantial girth and bowling ball size head.

"Does your head weigh sixteen pounds like a bowling ball," she jokingly inquired to Buster.

She looked at his dark face and imagined the eyes to be the two small holes for the fingers and his mouth the hole for the thumb. His head as tough and dense as the southern Florida lignum vitae hardwood tree the game balls were originally made from. Her husband used to collect the wooden spherical bowling balls produced before the 1900s, some small and without holes. However, they used the newer polyurethane balls, with more bounce, at the alley they used to manage.

She liked history. She was fascinated to learn where things originated. She looked at Buster stretched out on the floor in front of her. *Where had he come from?* She had been told they found him in a middle-class Albuquerque suburb.

Aunt June imagined he must have come from a nice family home. She wished he could speak English so he could tell her about his past. His disposition was gentle, and patient and he adored children. They must be heartbroken to have lost their friend.

When they went for walks around the trailer park, she would worry that someone might recognize him and tell his family where he was. She thought about getting a knock at the door by someone wanting to take him away. She found herself closing her curtains when they were home and jumping out of her chair with every knock at the front door.

A robust redheaded man sitting next to her finished rapidly texting on his phone using both his thick fingers with amazing dexterity.

"Hi there, are you going to Miami too?" She asked the man.

He didn't hear her speaking to him, so she asked again.

"Uh yea," he responded quickly looking back to the phone in his hands.

She watched Buster perk up by the loud zipping sound of the line barrier tape being sucked into its post after a man in an expensive suit stumbled into it after losing his footing. Then Buster became fixated on a small boy passing by, before whipping his head to look at a young woman wearing tall shiny knee-high black boots, who had been ogling him first. Aunt June attempted to smile at the young lady, but the girl only had eyes for Buster.

MARGOT STRUTTED the Las Vegas Airport concourse as if she were performing on the catwalk. Bluetooth concealed earbuds blasted hip-hop; Jay Z giving her an extra bounce to her step. Booming base tickled her insides. Her tall black leather boots clicked against the tile; her red knee-length skirt swished back and forth, feathering against her thighs, sans panties.

"No panties are my modus operandi," she would tell the boys with a wink.

Twenty-one-year-old Margot Melton was rocking her new hairstyle. Shaking her long blown out mane with golden highlights.

She spied a fit redhead hunk absorbed on his phone. It bothered her that he didn't seem to notice her.

"Men are only attracted to girls with long shiny hair," her mother would tell her. "I will never understand why any sane woman would want to look like a dyke with a short cut."

Approaching Gate 14, her almond shaped, brown eyes spotted an imposing silver Pitbull garbed in a red vest. Its long scratchy pink tongue was hanging from its mouth; a two-foot string of saliva dripped from the tip. Margot shivered feeling the tingling sensation shoot across her body.

"DGT!" Breathing out she attempted to calm the static energy forming from the flood of retrospection.

Don't Go There were the words she muttered when she wanted to quickly think of something else.

Margot's memories were compartmentalized into three groups: before memories started, Instagram memories, and DGT.

Margot had zero memories before the age of seven. Just a black hole in the space where others remembered birthday parties, playing dress up with friends, pretending with dolls, swimming in the ocean, and the family vacation to the Grand Canyon. She drew a blank when these events were mentioned, with only picture albums stored in the top of the hall closet as proof of her happy (at least on the surface) childhood. #happykids

Current memories were encapsulated into Instagram photo opts; #yogapose on the #sunsetbeach, wearing a #skimpy#stylish#bikini, reaching up to the sky under a pounding #waterfall, fine dining with her gorgeous #tan#stylishfriends#makingmemories, wearing a bohemian headscarf, beating on a drum, with a yellow-hued filter #bohemianchick, or napping with her man Brando #boyfriendandgirlfriend.

He was a powerfully photogenic hot model—the perfect Instagram boyfriend. Brando was a social influencer and showed her how to really increase her own following.

"If you put *#sustainable* on all your posts you will get thousands of additional followers," he said explaining what hash tags work best. "Keep the filters to a minimum, making sure to Photoshop a similar hue to get a more cohesive feel when you look at all the snaps together."

Margot hadn't seen Brando in over two months and was pretty sure he had been cheating on her while she was away in Vegas. She didn't judge him for that, having not been faithful herself. She was a young lady with an abnormal sexual desire. She frowned. Then looked for a seat nearer the gate that was not facing the dog.

Don't Go There thoughts started the day her memories began.

Skipping ahead...she started flashing boys indiscriminately in the eighth grade. She would expose her nipple, or slowly spread her legs to flash the boys, like the scene with Sharon Stone in *Basic Instinct,* except Margot was in schoolgirl uniform. #schoolgirlskirt

Trying to keep her thoughts on more neutral ground, after noticing the giant dog, she reminisced back to her junior high school crush on a shaggy, brown haired boy, Sam. She sent him mixed messages for weeks before inviting him home with her. He arrived at her house with a confident swagger. His jeans hung low off his hips to show the elastic of his American Eagle brand underwear. They were both performing an act, pretending to have done it all before. Joining them that day was his friend Ashley, a big boy on the lacrosse team; he would have been her backup crush if Sam hadn't worked out. They stood next to the peanut-shaped pool of her Coral Gables home. Fuchsia bougainvillea climbed the yellow stucco walls; the vines spreading over the trellised porch, leading out to the

Spanish tiled patio. Palm trees gently swayed in the salty breeze.

"Do you guys wanna take a dip?" Margot asked, kicking off her leather strappy sandals. "My mom and stepdad aren't around...they hardly ever are."

She turned on the Bose surround sound, connecting it to her iPhone; gangster rap bumped the energy up a notch. Margot sang the chorus, moving her small bony hips to the beat, grinding them against the air.

"Can you feel it? Uh-huh uhh, uh huh,"

"I didn't bring my swim trunks," Ashley said. "You should have told me this was a pool party."

"Nobody ever said you had to wear trunks...or anything at all," Margot bantered back.

He took off his shirt revealing his athletic physique, stripping down to his boxers and kicking off his jeans; they flew into the air landing on a yellow cushioned lounge chair.

"Banzai, motherfuckers!" Ashley hooted as he cannon-balled into the pool.

Water drenched Margot and Sam, cooling them instantly in the thick Miami heat.

"My feet are burning!" She said hopping back and forth on the hot terra cotta tile.

She slipped off her blouse, with her distressed jean shorts dropping to the ground, she danced around in her white lace bra and panties, before running and jumping into the peanut-shaped pool. Sam was already diving in behind her. He lurched up and grabbed her from behind. Flirtatiously they started splashing one another wildly, moving towards the diving board. Ashley began swimming lengths of the pool, beneath the water, holding his breath. Under the rectangle shade of the board Sam started to kiss her, apprehensively reaching his hand out to caress her small breast. She could feel his bulge rubbing against her own throbbing space and wanted it so bad; pulling her hips to him, she wrapped her legs around his waist. His soft wet lips covered her mouth.

They heard the door slam shut and immediately pulled away from each other. Her mother walked onto the patio, wearing skintight white designer Juicy Couture jeans, with a gold belt, tangerine silk tank top, with sizable gold-hooped earrings, accentuated against her long brown hair. #juicy-cougar #sustainable

"Do you mind if I join you?" Her mother asked the teens, standing at the edge of the pool. "Who are your friends, Margot?"

Margot introduced the boys to her mother, before Alison followed by the family dog, an impressive pit named Hugo, went to change into her bikini. Sam smiled causing his cute freckles to dance across his nose.

"Is your mom okay with us being here?" He splashed her and grinned flirtatiously, "Are you being a bad girl?"

"Alison is cool, as long as you aren't a woman married to a wealthy man. Alison is a man-grabber. She'll snatch a husband and blow a family's house down before you say B.I.T.C.H."

The dog returned following her mother. Choosing to plop his heavy body down in the shade of the covered patio. Hugo let out a deep breath of resignation and closed his eyes to the sun. Her mother began setting up her chair with a thick yellow terry cloth towel, iced beverage, her designer sunglasses, romance novel, cover up shirt, the entire time gabbing to Ashley about what was happening to so and so at the club.

Ashley was relaxed, with his arms crossed over the pool ledge, while Alison quizzed him, "Who are your parents

Ashley...do I know them...what does your father do for a living?"

Sam swam closer to Margot and started to poke her with his big toe. Margot grabbed the digit, and rubbed it against her cunt, through the bathing suit. Sam's face showed building excitement, she took it a step further, and moved the suit to the side. He pushed against the edge of the pool to leverage himself, penetrating her with the big digit. They both took a deep breath and she started to move up and down—while her mother droned on about the club.

"What are you guys doing over there?" Ashley turned to look towards the diving board and address the horny hush.

"Just playing footsie," Sam smirked. #toesucking #sustainable

---

Today Margot was returning to Miami to see her mother. Las Vegas hadn't been as good to her as she had expected.

She had tried to find work that paid a decent salary and didn't make her want to barf. Margot was offered work as the receptionist at a tanning bed salon at a strip mall. The job paid $8.50 an hour for her to wipe sweaty skin, mixed with greasy lotion, off warm beds. Then she started a second part-time job selling jewelry at Dillard's department store in a suburban shopping mall. Working both jobs, she could barely cover the rent, much less afford to go clubbing, the main reason she had moved to Vegas. The best DJs played the Vegas Strip—these nightclubs charged a $40 cover—she was too poor to dance, unless she got a job stripping at the Palomino Club.

A few days ago, her mother had called to inform Margot that she was embattled in her third divorce and needed to move out of the house with the peanut-shaped pool to a condo on the beach. Margot knew this was her way out.

"I'm coming home to help, mom," she told Alison over the phone.

"Margot don't worry about it," her mom quickly interjected. "I'm already dating the next contender. This new man has twice the money."

Margot knew she had better claim her spot at the beach condo before her mom married again.

Her mother lived by her own rules, professing, "If you want to be happy for the rest of your life—don't marry for love—don't marry for looks—marry for money."

"I'll get the first ticket to Miami," Margot had told her mom. #beachcondo #sustainable

Margot sat with her long legs crossed, tapping one black-heeled boot impatiently against the other bootleg, waiting for the dead battery on her iPhone to charge in the port under the seat. She sat observing people near the boarding area, waiting for the fourth group to be called, on account her assigned seat was in front of the economy section.

Two well dressed, middle-aged men, walked up to the first-class pre-boarding line; a tan attractive woman, seemingly irritated, followed behind pulling two pieces carry-on of luggage. The man in the designer suit stumbled over the metal pole barrier, and then a loud zipping sound emitted from the line separation tape, as it disconnected from the post he had knocked. Nobody seemed to regard the drunken first-class passengers. #drunkoldmen #sustainable

Those waiting to board remained engrossed on their iPhones and computer screens. She redirected her attention to a woman with long brown hair worn in a braid over her shoulder; she was holding a small baby, loaded down with baggage, she looked the part of a Nepalese Sherpa, while attempting to guide a loose toddler along the pre-boarding path.

A knot formed in Margot's throat, like she had swallowed a fly, when she again spotted the big silver dog, calmly waiting on the other side of the partitioned off boarding groups. His amber eyes were fixated on the man in the suit who had made the loud noise. It held its gaze on the man until he disappeared down the corridor. A little boy went skipping past, and like a squirrel running up a tree, dragged the big dog's attention away. The boy slowed down and started to reach out for the animal, before his mother said something to stop him, guiding him towards the waiting agent. The silver dog continued to watch the child intently. Absorbed with small boy's animated movements, as he rolled on the ground, before handing over his ticket to the gate agent.

Then, for no apparent reason, the dog snapped its neck to face her; locking his unwavering yellow eyes with Margot's almond shaped ones. The dog knew she had been watching it. The hairs on the back of her neck stood at attention. Goose pimples popped from her skin, like the sudden onset of the measles. She felt sick.

"ARE YOU ENJOYING PEOPLE WATCHING BUSTER?" Aunt June asked me.

My eyes looked up at her sitting in the extra-wide handicap seat in the waiting area of the airport. I was resting on the floor with my heavy head between my paws, my back legs stretched out straight behind me. I was very much enjoying watching people.

I had been surprised when a woman smelling of jasmine flowers ran over my paws with her suitcase, while busy connecting with a man smiling back at her wearing a matching uniform. She hadn't seen me as she hurried along, with my fur matching the short dark gray carpet. She jumped back startled. I stood up quickly in response, even though it didn't hurt in the slightest.

I was happy when the lady spoke to me with concern in her voice afterwards.

"I'm sorry buddy."

Raising her pitch to complement me, she said, "I love your cactus collar handsome boy. Are you from the desert?"

I panted with a giant grin. My eyebrows raised; my interest peaked.

"He's the friendliest dog in the world," Aunt June informed her.

The sweet-scented woman patted my bolder-sized head.

My attention kept getting dragged from one interesting sight to another, human smells converging with each other. The zipping sound of the rope being retracted after a man in a dark suit bumped it fascinated me. I could smell the alcohol seeping from under his suit, permeating off his skin. And the tall jovial man accompanying him smelled equally of intoxication and newly purchased clothing.

Out of nowhere, a child began to reach out to touch me, I could hardly contain my excitement. My bottom end began zigzagging out of control while I held my place waiting for his sticky fingers to caress me. *Oh boy!*

"Blake don't touch that dog," his mother demanded him.

Like a balloon I was deflated, my bum wiggled to a stop as I watched him run down the corridor.

I felt the purr of human energy directed at me and turned my head to locate the vibration. A young woman was staring at me. I took her in, watching as she tapped her black leather boots together with a deep-seated agitation. She reminded of me of a cat woman—the boots her sharp claws. I sniffed at the air and smelled her leather boots.

Aunt June resituated herself. She began to gather her belongings; with exaggerated effort pulling her fuzzy peach sweater over her flowery dress and placing her plastic water bottle into her purse. Her preparation made me aware that it was about time to board the airplane.

I thought about my training to be a Service Dog with Cindy.

"We will be testing his alertness in each of the following situations: in a person's home, in a person's yard, including a vehicle, in a store, office building, mall, airport, or in an outdoor location, such as a park," she explained to Aunt June. "Or, anywhere that is unfamiliar to the dog. Noisy distractions will include people talking, running, people in uniforms, cars, animals, loud machinery, sirens and hidden food."

Having accomplished all the obstacles with flying colors I realized I had never been on an airplane. This was unfamiliar territory. I repositioned myself back on the floor fully attentive. I was feeling excited, I wondered what the plane would smell like. *Oh boy!*

I noticed a redheaded man sitting two seats over from Aunt June flexing his bicep muscles, then twitching his chest muscles, back and forth, right to left. I wondered if I could twitch my muscles and stood back up to sit on my behind.

I began to flex my chest. The muscles quivered.

A woman reeking of pharmaceuticals and oozing depression ambled by us. Her long stringy hair made a mop down her back. I saw Aunt June try and shoot her a smile. It was ignored.

I flexed my muscles.

YOU LUCKY DOG

SHE USED to sit in first class with her husband before the divorce. Now she was assigned 13F—a window seat in the economy section—alone as usual. She heaved her shiny purple, carry-on luggage, into the above compartment. Awkwardly squeezing her two-hundred-pound body into the far seat.

"I hope I don't have to pee," she had suffered from incontinence, following the birth of her youngest, Ryan.

"After Ryan was born, I could never jump on a trampoline again," she used to tell her mom friends at the playgroups.

After Ryan was born everything changed.

Barberella couldn't keep the weight off. She stuck mostly with counting calories using the Weight Watchers program; losing the weight, just to have it come back the next year, plus an extra ten pounds. She was seduced by the Paleo fad diet, choosing to cut all carbohydrates from the family meal plan for several years.

"Let's eat like cavemen," she told her husband.

He agreed to the carnivorous diet, quickly losing twenty

pounds and keeping it off. Her weight came back within the year. Leaving her body more engorged and bloated than ever.

"It wouldn't have been so hard if I had been a homely girl," she had cried to her therapist.

Proliferating her plight was that Barberella had been Miss Texas 1992. Her thick blond hair fell down her back in soft bouncy curls...before falling out in handfuls from her thyroid and hormonal issues. She dreaded brushing her hair, forced to watch the horse bristles yank the loose strands from her head. In front of the mirror, Barberella would focus her attention on the thinning part-line, highlighted by her white scalp, anything to avoid looking too closely at deepening wrinkles on her middle-aged face. Two parallel lines between her eyebrows had indented a permanent scowl.

Barberella had always dreamed of being a wife and mother. After graduating from high school with high academic scores, and even better, as the captain of the drill team, she set her ambitions on attending Texas A&M for two years. Her purpose was to meet her future husband. She certainly had no intentions of earning a degree, with no plans to work outside the home in her future. Her prayers were answered when she met John during her second year at college, the same year she won Miss Texas 1992. Having bagged the beauty pageant title—her marriage to John was a done deal—mission accomplished.

His smell was intoxicating. She would inhale the space between his neck and collarbone like a cocaine addict. He had dreamy blue eyes with long dark eyelashes. Barberella wanted her kids to have John's eyes. She had blue eyes too. With genetics answering her prayers, Mazy came out a gorgeous blue-eyed mix of her parents. Two years later, Ryan was born with those same dazzling blue eyes.

Two years after that, Barberella still hadn't lost the last twenty pregnancy pounds remaining on her petite form. Her husband didn't look at her anymore.

She remembered watching him grab his sports bag from the top shelf of their overstuffed walk-in closet, aggressively shoving his squash-racket into the canvas.

"What time will you be home tonight?"

"I really don't know, Barb." He seemed irritated. "I'll let you know when I know." Out of nowhere he stopped packing his bag. Pausing for a moment. His blue eyes turned cruel. "I've decided I don't want any more children with you."

Barberella wanted three children. Hearing this she jerked her body back; a quasi-whale being hit by an icebreaker ship.

"You promised me we would have another baby!"

"Okay, Barb," John sneered taking a moment to look her up and down. "Two can play that game...you duped me into thinking you were a beauty queen."

From that day forward, she desperately pleaded with him whenever he was home.

"Please love me, John, like you used to...come home for dinner tonight. I'm begging you...think about your family... think about me."

"No wonder I don't want to be home," he would disparage her groveling at his feet.

He begrudgingly stayed with her until the day after Mazy's high school graduation. John had planned it all out. He had packed his clothes and favorite belongings, leaving a note for her to read on the kitchen counter.

She hadn't noticed the letter on the marble island countertop when she returned from the grocery store. She had been busy unloading the groceries and then folding and storing the reusable canvas bags in the pantry. Letting her mind wander, she was thinking about the beautiful rack of lamb with mint jelly she was serving for dinner, and the perfect Spanish Rioja wine she had paired with it, when she spotted the letter on the counter. It was written with quick scratchy scrawl on the monogrammed notepaper she had gifted John for Christmas.

Dear Barberella,

You knew this was coming, so don't act surprised. You are as much to blame as me. I will send a moving company to collect my belongings in the next week. Let's be civil about this. We still have Ryan to think about. If you make this divorce process easy, Ryan can stay with you. If you make trouble, I will make sure you never see him again. It is time to move on.

Regards,

John

After reading the letter, she vomited her Starbucks latte into the island sink. Resting her swollen age-spotted hands on the cool gray marble. Her large solitaire diamond winked at her.

She heard footsteps upstairs. Ryan was at school. Mazy was in Arizona with her girlfriends attending a graduation party. Barberella realized the possibility that John was still in the house at the same moment he came around the corner and stepped into the kitchen. They locked blue eyes. He looked down at the "Dear John letter" she was holding in her quivering hand. He sniffed the air, smelling her puke.

"I take it you read the note," he said. "I didn't plan on being here, but I forgot something."

She began to drown, sputtering for a breath, in the ocean of his deep blue eyes. He had to still love her. They had made a family together. She was infatuated with him.

"Please don't go," she said as tears began running down her face, her forehead wrinkling in disillusion. "I knew you were unhappy, but I didn't think you would leave me. I've tried so hard to be beautiful, to make a perfect home for you. Can we go to counseling? Please John don't go!"

Barberella was crying desperately, taking small shallow breaths. She couldn't grasp the oxygen she needed. She felt her face and hands and heart burning hot. She was begging him. John started to walk around the island to the garage door, heading for his parked car. She followed behind him as he opened the door. Dropping to her knees, she grabbed him by his leg, burying her face into his crotch, taking in the smell of lust for the last time. Holding him to her she pleaded.

"Just talk to me...give me another chance...look at me John!"

He answered these imploring demands by looking down at her, his sadistic eyes simmered—two dark festering holes in her universe. Small bits of spittle formed on his lower lip. She watched his nostrils flare with his heavy breaths.

"Nobody wants you Barberella...I don't want you...your children don't want you...and your friends don't want you. Nobody wants you Barberella. Let go of me."

He wiped her off dismissively like an annoying fly. She sunk her fleshy body into the white marble floor. John slammed the car door, making her flinch like a kick to the gut. She listened to the electric motor rolling the garage door closed. Followed by unbearable silence.

The airplane seatbelt was pulled as large as it would go and barely fit.

"This is ridiculous...I'm not that fat."

She imagined having to ask the flight attendant for the seat belt extension.

"Just when you thought it couldn't get any worse, Barberella." She laughed out loud at her own dark humor.

She was aware that she no longer fit the regular sizes sold in department clothing stores, having surpassed the extra-large size fourteen. She used to be a size four. So, if she did the math and multiplied twenty pounds by five dress sizes, she had put on a whopping hundred pounds on her petite frame.

"A large bag of dog food weighs thirty-five pounds," the Weight-Watchers group leader had explained to her at a meeting once. "Imagine carrying all that weight on your back and knees every day."

She sat locked in her seat, with her thin stringy blond hair cascading over her ample bosom. She wished the middle seat would remain empty. Barberella hoped she wouldn't do anything embarrassing during the flight. On a flight she had taken several months ago to visit her son, she took two prescribed Xanax before eating a saltine cracker. Waking upon landing, she realized she hadn't finished the cracker completely before falling asleep; it remained partially chewed in her open mouth. The man and his daughter sitting next to her had tried to ignore Barberella, as she roused herself from her comatose state with the slimy cracker mush caked to her lips and cheeks.

A brown leather Coach bag sat on her lap. It was the same purse she carried before the divorce, but now the gold buckles had tarnished, and the leather was worn. Unzipping the bag, she reached inside a pocket to pull out a small gold pillbox decorated with roses and then cracked the lid off a newly purchased bottle of Evian water. The pillbox contained the Xanax she required for the flight; the prescription said to take two pills. She would skip the cracker this time, she thought smiling to herself.

Barberella looked up from her window seat to see an older woman with frizzy white hair limping slowly, with the help of a cane. A massive silver dog sidekick, wearing a red service dog vest, was leading her.

"Halt, Buster," the woman's unsteady voice shook.

The old lady looked around, squinting her eyes behind thick spectacles, to locate her and Buster's seats. One row diagonally behind Barberella, the elderly woman motioned for the big dog to jump into the middle seat. The dog looked as wide as its owner.

"I wonder if HE fits in the seat?" Barberella said to the empty seats surrounding her.

An exceptionally beautiful flight attendant arrived to assist the dog's disabled owner with her luggage. The stewardess stretched her thin body to store the woman's plastic Target bag in the compartment above.

"I'm Carmen," she told the woman. "You just push the call button if you need any further assistance."

Barberella wished they wouldn't allow dogs on planes. It seemed like they were shoving the word "companion" in her face. John had been kind enough to leave the family's mammoth size Great Pyrenees mountain dog, Pumpkin, at the ranch when he moved out.

John gifted Pumpkin to the children at Christmas seven years prior to leaving her. The white puppy came in a giant box, glittering in silver and red-striped paper, with a jumbo velvet red bow. The kids squealed in delight when a *real* fluffy white teddy bear popped out.

John allowed Barberella to stay at the Texas ranch for two years following the divorce, so Ryan could complete high school, the contract stated, after which John would either have the option to purchase Barberella's half of the property, or they would sell the ranch, splitting the profits. She was unable to afford the million-dollar Texas ranch on a housewife's, or in her case a jobless person's salary. She had nothing to lean on, with no job prospects. Zero references. Zero experience. She knew she was screwed. The worst part was that she had signed the divorce agreement in such an absent state of mind that Pumpkin had been part of the bargain. John was to get her best friend when he bought her out.

───────

Barberella closed her eyes, thinking about her daughter Mazy's sunset beach wedding tomorrow afternoon in Key West. The invite said not to wear shoes. She would see John and his new thirty-year-old fiancé Callie. Sweet little Mazy, with her big blue eyes had begged her mom not to make a scene. John and the replacement bitch already lived together at the ranch—Barberella's family ranch. The couple had recently brought home a new puppy; a fluffy white nine-week-old female Great Pyrenees they named

Nellie. She saw the pictures on Facebook after Mazy had been tagged.

Barberella pulled out her noise-canceling headphones and turned the switch on, placing the cushioned earpieces over her thinning blond hair. *Aw*, total silence. She dug around in her purse and again pulled out the flowered gold pillbox. With the little strength left, she flipped the lid open and popped one more Xanax.

THINGS USUALLY TURNED out well for Dee. Today, however, she felt abandoned by her good friend, Lady Luck. Serendipity having chosen to stay behind in the Vegas casino—it wasn't in the cards—with Dee barely making her return flight to Miami.

Following other passengers, she took baby steps down the aisle, seeking seat 14D, somewhere near the front of coach.

"Oh, Crap," she sighed, finally surrendering herself to the resistant day.

The assigned aisle seat was going to be a problem. Sitting in the row next to hers, was an old woman with frizzy white hair, and a goddamn giant Pitbull. It sat in the middle seat wearing an official looking red vest. Dee was mad dogging the dog, when she noticed it was also watching her, smiling from ear to ear, mimicking its owner's chirpy disposition in the adjacent seat.

Dee was allergic. Not to old people, but to dogs. She wouldn't die from her allergy to animal dander, but by the time she arrived in Miami, she was going to be a snotty mess, unable to breathe through her nose and suffering from a pounding headache. She already had a hangover from the Vegas bachelorette party she had attended the night before. Now she needed to return to Miami for work the next morning. Dee would be covered in large red hives if she didn't remove herself from the plane immediately. She started to turn around, in order to weave her way back to the front galley and inform the flight attendant of her problem. A line of passengers had already stacked up behind her. She was forced to lower herself temporarily into the assigned spot, cramming her tote in the storage space under the seat in front of her to wait for the remaining passengers to be situated.

Dee looked to her left, accidentally catching the eye of the old woman who was still smiling at her. She returned a dispirited smirk, looking down at her hands, while trying to avoid eye contact with the woman. She didn't want to talk to anyone, much less some sweet old lady, causing her to take a later flight.

"Hi honey," the old woman said with a shaky voice. "You look like you're having a bad day."

Dee stared back at the old woman, then peered down at the coffee stains splattered across the breast of her white t-shirt.

It had been one of those days. Some would call it a bad day. Dee didn't like to think in such extremes as good or bad—black or white—it always seemed to work out for her either way.

She had to rush to the airport this morning, almost missing her flight. The alarm had mistakenly been set for

6pm—not 6am. She only woke after hearing one of the other lady's tiptoeing into the shared hotel suite. As her late night, party animal friend knocked into a dresser, the noise from a lamp crashing roused Dee from her deep sleep. Realizing the time, she quickly ripped on her faded jeans and a white t-shirt. Her slept-on brown hair was a rat's nest, with bobby pins sticking out from each angle. This messy hairdo was the complete opposite to her usual meticulous clean-cut style.

Before leaving the hotel, she had noticed her Florida driver's license wasn't in the correct clear plastic pocket of her organized wallet. She must have misplaced it celebrating her friend Marne's bachelorette party on the Vegas Strip the night before, joining with a group of girlfriends from her college days to take ecstasy pills and wash them down with shots of tequila.

"What happens in Vegas...stays in Vegas!" The ladies slurred while shrieking with laughter.

Dee wasn't a prude, although she opted out of the wet t-shirt contest to everyone's disappointment. She did choose to participate in riding the mechanical bull. Dee stopped drinking alcohol after finishing her fourth vodka-grapefruit Greyhound cocktail, finishing the night hydrating with water, and burning off the liquor by booty grinding with a hot guy from New Jersey. His shaved smooth body had sported a lime-green muscle shirt and a thick gold chain.

She tore the room apart searching for the missing ID; shaking the contents out of her clutch handbag, then pulling out the pockets of the sequined black pants she had worn the night before. Not having any luck, and with no time to waste, she grabbed her bags and ran down to the lobby and out the front doors of the Aria Casino and Hotel. She dashed across the nearly empty Las Vegas Boulevard, heading into a mall along the Strip, to locate the bar with the mechanical bull.

She ran past the darkened Victoria's Secret, American Outfitters, and Sketchers stores, passing numerous closed booths advertising cell phone cases or ponytail wigs and hair-pieces. When she found the bar with the bull, she noticed everything had been put away; chairs were stacked on the tables and the lights were turned off. She could hear muffled voices coming from in the bar. The quiet was a stark contrast to the thundering bass pumping a few hours earlier. But this was Vegas baby—luckily, she found a few workers still sitting at the bar. Dee remembered one of the men from a few hours earlier.

"Morning. Any way you guys found an ID last night?"

The bartender, who she had recognized, stood up and moved slowly to the cash register. He pushed a couple of buttons and the drawer shot out in front of him. He reached in and plucked out her ID.

"I figured you would be back—just not so soon," he smiled with a toothpick stuck between his teeth; dark circles had formed under his eyes from the all-night shift. "It was jammed between the vinyl booths in the back. You're lucky I found it."

"Lucky...that's hard to say," Dee pinched the ID between her fingers, swiftly replacing it into the correct clear pocket on the outside of her wallet. "I still have to catch my plane."

She was able to hail a cab a split-second after exiting the mall. Upon arriving at the airport, she had less than one hour remaining to check her bag and pass through TSA.

"No time for coffee," she groaned. "Darn it!"

Then she saw a mousy barista with a tray full of free sample lattes, cappuccinos, and berry smoothies. She grabbed the baby-sized latte, feeling lucky to have the miniature caffeine dose. Impulse from the night before caused Dee to take the mini latte like a shot of tequila. However, she hesitated for a second at the prospect of the hot liquid burning her pallet. Missing the target. Espresso and milk dripped down her chin covering her white t-shirt with brown coffee splatters.

"Here honey," the barista handing her a napkin. "Take another sample drink—not your lucky day."

"I'm going to need all the luck I can get," Dee lamented as she dabbed the napkin against her stained shirt. "I still have to catch my plane."

She counted thirty people standing in the TSA queue in front of her. She checked her pink swatch; it was 7:35am and the plane departed at 8am. She realized it was going to be too close for comfort.

Dee watched an obese TSA officer slowly amble to the front of the long line. The man was bulging from his uniform as he reached to pull the line divider strap across to where Dee stood, altering the TSA route. He then motioned for Dee to follow him the other direction. He turned to the people behind her and told them to form a new line behind Dee.

"You get to be at the head of the line," the heavy breathing TSA agent informed her.

He licked his lips the full-monty, with his creepy mustache twisting to say, "It's your lucky day." The fat agent checked to see if the name on her ticket matched her ID, passing her through. She took off her shoes, belt, and jacket, putting them into the tray next to her purse. Then she proceeded through the body scanner X-ray machine. Raising her hands into the air and out to the sides of her head, then turning around to make eye contact with the next official manning the scanner exit.

"Please step out from the scanner and stand in front of me," the TSA agent promptly demanded.

A woman officer in a navy uniform walked towards them snapping on her blue rubber gloves. She explained to Dee that she was going to perform a body check.

"Would you prefer a private room?" The woman asked the disheveled Dee.

Dee shook her head back and forth, signaling *no* nervously.

The female officer rubbed her gloved hands up the inside of her thighs, patted her buttocks, pushing up to the armpits to trace Dee's breasts with her plastic palm. The stranger finished off with a nod of approval. Dee took off running in her untied shoes, her belt in one hand, straight for the departure gate, just as she heard the last call for those boarding Flight 982, traveling from Las Vegas to Miami.

"What is your name?" The frizzy haired old woman asked Dee. "You can call me Aunt June and this is Buster, we are pleased to meet you. Tell her 'Hi' Buster."

The dog nodded its bowling ball head, as if he understood what she was saying, lifting one of his white paws to wave hello.

It certainly didn't feel like lady luck had her back today. After the remaining passengers had been seated, Dee reached above her head and pressed the call button. Moments later an attractive Cuban flight attendant answered the lighted button by pushing it off.

"What can I do for you?" Asked the attendant as she leaned in towards Dee.

Carmen was printed on her nametag. Dee responded quietly to her inquiry, trying not to make a scene.

"Hi Carmen...um...I guess I have a problem," Dee said half-heartedly.

She then pointed to the smiling silver dog across the aisle.

"I'm actually allergic to dogs."

Carmen's pseudo smile faded. The attendant looked to the big canine. The dog was also examining her with alert yellow eyes.

"Can I move you to the back of the plane ma'm?" Carmen coaxed Dee. "We have plenty of seating available far away from the dog."

Dee could already feel the irritation building in her nose and elsewhere.

"I'm allergic, Carmen, from everywhere on the plane."

Dee pointed at a married couple taking their seats a few rows towards the front. The man held a small carrier with yellow fluff busting out the round holes.

"And look at those people with their little dog!" Dee said a bit excitedly.

"Well I'm sorry I can't ask them to leave the plane as they are paying customers too."

Dee knew not to make an issue of it. The big dog wasn't paying for his flight. The YouTube video with the Asian doctor being dragged off the plane by security, with blood dripping from his face, came to mind. She bent over to pick up her tote.

Carmen stood with her back straight, adjusting her uniform sweater vest.

"I have no doubt that we can get you on the next plane

leaving Las Vegas. How about we collect your belongings and walk you to customer service to take care of this unfortunate situation."

The old lady, Aunt June, gave Dee a sympathetic look when she stood up to gather the rest of her things. She had a pretty good book to read while she waited for the next flight to Miami. She started to look forward to getting a Grande coffee and maybe she could steal a power nap in one of those comfy Starbucks' chairs she had spotted while rushing to her flight.

The flight attendant followed her down the aisle.

"If you're lucky you might even get an upgrade for your trouble, Miss Winn."

Several rows ahead she nearly stepped on a small toy airplane discarded on the aisle floor. Dee bent to pick up the plastic miniature. As she stood, she locked eyes with a beautiful little boy, freckles scattered across his button nose. The child wore a long sleeved striped red and blue shirt that matched the airplane she held in her hand.

"Is this yours?" Dee asked him, holding out the model airplane on her open palm.

The child smiled brightly reaching to grasp the toy with his dimpled fingers.

"Fanks wady," he spat through his gapped smile. "It's my wucky day."

Carmen had worked with her friend Nicco many times with both flight attendants claiming Miami as their home base. They lived in South Beach only a few blocks from one another. It was a twenty-minute walk to the beach; with sidewalk patio restaurants, pastel painted boutique shops, art deco hotels, and palm trees pulsating with the sweet Latin music that burst from flashy convertibles.

Carmen rarely joined him for his weekend romps at the clubs, instead she chose to live vicariously through his outrageous post-party stories.

Nicco was scurrying about the service area at the front of the plane, holding a pen in one hand, as he marked items off the departure checklist. Carmen continued to greet the final passengers boarding the airplane, welcoming them to the friendly skies with her captivating smile and mascara brushed, twinkling gray eyes.

A frail thin man stepped over the threshold, entering the plane holding a dog carrier. Yellow fur was popping out the holes of the crate. When he smiled, she unconsciously recoiled from the shock at seeing the right side of his face was missing. Behind him a lovely, petite woman, dressed in a buttoned periwinkle shirt and matching capris, pulled a robin's egg hued piece of luggage behind her. Carmen recovered quickly from her initial response to the man and then overcompensated by shining even brighter. She quickly darted her eyes from his deformed face to focus on the feather light woman in blue.

"Welcome to Freedom Airlines, can I help you find your seats?"

"We're in row 12B and C," the bird-like woman chirped. "I think we can find it."

"Ma'am...eh...sir," Carmen mumbled while holding her smile firm. "The plane is only half full, so the window seat in your row is available, please make yourselves comfortable."

After the couple was directed to their seats, she helped the last two people to board, a young teenage girl and her father, by showing them their assigned seats at the front of coach. Then she returned to help Nicco restock the remaining essentials: napkins, straws, juice, and pretzel packs, before they secured everything for take-off.

"Girl, I'm so happy we're working together," Nicco squealed and clapped his hands together. "We're going to have some fun today! Did you see who was in first class? Oh my God. The one and only Senator Young...is...on...this flight."

Carmen raised her groomed eyebrows.

"Senator?"

"Oh, Carmen, come on honey. You don't know who he is? Oh well. It's best you don't care about it all anyway. It would just put your panties in a wad—he has mine. We won't have to deal with him since we're working economy, anyways."

Carmen hated politics.

"Move on, Nicco," she whispered under her breath.

"Do you want me to do the safety announcement?" Nicco asked her as they walked down the aisle towards the back of the plane. Both flight attendants began closing the storage compartments and checking that passengers had placed their baggage correctly under the seats in front of them.

"You know...the passengers would prefer YOU give them the safety show!" He buttered her.

Carmen plucked the yellow demo bag from the upper compartment at the back of the plane. She puckered her lips with her freshly applied red lipstick, posing like it was a glamour shot, giving Nicco a sultry look, sticking her small, curved hip out to the side, with her hands on her waist.

"Show time!" She winked.

"Girl...with you it's always magic!"

Carmen heard the *bing* of the call light; it looked to be row 14D. She walked fixedly towards a flustered messy haired woman who had pressed the button. The woman explained how she had a dog allergy and pointed out the Pitbull next to her and then pointed at the Pomeranian several rows up. Carmen could tell the young woman knew the airline rules about individuals suffering from allergies.

"You should have called the airline to confirm that no dogs were on the flight," she informed the woman.

Then offered her a different seat away from the animals. The frazzled woman vehemently refused.

"Ma'am," Carmen started.

"My name is Dee Winn. I didn't know I was supposed to call ahead."

Carmen cleared her throat and began again.

"The airline allows for two pets in first class, two in

business, and four in the main cabin. However, both dogs you have pointed out are service animals. By law we must accommodate them at no charge. There is no limit on the number of service animals aboard the aircraft," Carmen explained to the woman. "I'm sorry there is nothing I can do for you. Let's see if we can get you on the next flight."

Carmen helped gather Miss Winn's bag to further assist her off the plane. In doing so, she turned to the frizzy haired Aunt June and the big dog, Buster, sitting across the aisle and gave them a sympathetic look.

Carmen never really liked dogs. She was more of a cat person.

"Cats are as smart as dogs," her veterinarian had informed her. "It's a fact."

She assumed the negative opinion of dogs was acquired when she was ten years old, from her father's brother, Uncle Silvio. She remembered his skinny figure standing in cut-off jeans, with grease stained fingers wrapped around a Natural Ice beer can. He was always griping in Spanish about the stray dogs running around the Little Havana neighborhood; getting into the trash, menacing the children, and fighting with each other.

"Los perros están corriendo por las calles," he would grumble to anyone who would listen to his slang-filled Spanish. "Los perros estarán muertos para mañana!"

He made a slicing motion across his neck when he made the decision to kill the dogs.

She didn't like the menacing dogs running the streets either. They encroached on her ability to play outside. She was too afraid to walk to her friend Mabel's house around the corner because of the free roaming animals. Uncle Silvio decided the best way to remedy the stray dog population was by poisoning the free dogs, along with any owned dogs that got in the way that night.

He went to the Winn Dixie grocery store and purchased a discounted package of rib-eye steaks from the meat department. He took the raw steaks to his shed at the back of the property; where he kept his MAC tools, fishing equipment, tarps, all his car parts, oil, lubes, antifreeze and pesticides. Her uncle chopped the steaks into large pieces, drenching them in Malathion, a pesticide that kills insects by preventing their nervous system from working properly. He spread the chunks of poisoned meat throughout the neighborhood. Some pieces he placed near the garbage bins the dogs frequented. He doled out the scraps in the alleyways behind restaurants and businesses. He set several tainted portions around the perimeter of the Fuentes' residence.

The next day havoc erupted in the community. Dead dogs lay indisposed in the hibiscus bushes, near the dumpsters, and sprawled on the cracked sidewalks leading to people's homes. Some dogs were foaming from their mouths, struggling to kick their nerve damaged paws. One of the ill-fated dogs that suffered through the night was Carmen's friend Mabel's Labrador-mix, Fido. Mabel cried to her about the loss of her furry companion over the phone the next day.

"I let him out, Carmen," Mabel blamed herself, blubbering over her own words. "The back gate was open... he was scratching at the door like someone was out back and he like wanted to check it out. I just let him out. He ate the poisoned meat...that someone left outside to murder him with!"

Carmen cringed while holding back the family secret from her friend.

A freaky fate later met her Uncle Silvio; she believed it was bad karma created from the dog killings. Her uncle Silvio had invited his best drinking buddy to the shed at the back of the property. He wanted to share in libation with a batch of his homemade wine. The bottles weren't labeled. A prior day while drunk, her Uncle Silvio had consolidated the concentrated Malathion poison into an identical bottle to the bottles of wine. Without realizing it he grabbed the wrong container.

"I think it went bad Silvio...it tastes like shit!" Uncle Silvio's friend spit out the nasty tasting liquid.

Uncle Silvio wasn't having it. He had worked hard making the wine and was insulted by his friend's negative response. He took a big swig from the bottle, guzzling down the foul-tasting drink, too proud to admit the wine tasted off. His friend decided to head home after drinking the questionable beverage.

"Hasta la vista, Silvio."

He loaded into his rusted Ford pickup truck and drove about a mile before he felt nauseated and began vomiting. Causing the pickup truck to veer off the road going thirty miles per hour, hitting a palm tree. Steam pouring from the collapsed engine. When the paramedics pulled Silvio's friend from the vehicle, he had begun to suffer muscle tremors, cramps, shortness of breath, a slowed heart rate, headache, abdominal pain and diarrhea. The Malathion had traveled to his liver and kidneys affecting his nervous system. Vomit covered the front of his shirt as he slipped in and out of consciousness. Uncle Silvio's friend later woke in the ICU, immediately bombarded with questions from the doctors.

"Are you suicidal? What did you eat? Where were you coming from? Was there anyone else who ingested the poison?"

His friend explained that it was Uncle Silvio who had given him the tainted wine before he had crashed his truck into the palm tree. The police rushed to Carmen's family's pastel green home. Carmen watched from her bedroom window as the uniformed officers headed directly to the shed in the backyard. They found Uncle Silvio sprawled out on the dirt floor as dead as the dogs he had killed.

The big silver Pitbull seemed like he was a nice enough animal, Carmen figured. He was wearing an official looking red vest.

She had heard passengers exclaiming to its owner, Aunt June, "Your dog is so cute and well behaved!"

The fuzzy little yapper Pomeranian was another story. People would complain during the flight about its incessant barking, no doubt.

A BARKING DOG SELDOM BITES

WHEN EZRA and her daddy stepped past the first-class separation wall upon boarding, she spotted the ferocious looking gray dog, sitting seven rows behind her. It was too close. She felt the comforting weight of her daddy's warm hands placed on her shoulders. He squeezed, clutching the right shoulder a little tighter, directing her to their assigned seats at the front of coach.

She had been so concerned about the massive dog upon entering the economy section, she hardly noticed the man with a silver ponytail walking only inches in front of her, before he suddenly twisted his body to the side, swinging around a dog crate he held in his right hand. In it, a feisty yellow mongrel growled. Surprised by the animal so close to her comfort zone, she took a step back. The weight of her backpack pulled her off balance, causing her to fall against her daddy. Like a superhero he transformed instantly into a protective padded wall.

Grrrrrr...Yip...Yip...Yip. The kenneled Pomeranian was ferociously growling and barking at the shaken Ezra.

"Bruno. No barking," the ponytailed man scolded the obnoxious mutt.

Ezra was so frightened she hardly noticed the man's slurred speech impediment from a face deformity. The man looked back at the frightened girl being comforted by her father and awkwardly slurred an apology to them.

"Excuse my naughty dog. I'm sorry for that," she thought he said.

The man maneuvered the dog crate in front of him, and then continued four rows back, before finding their seats.

"That dog is even closer than the big dog, daddy."

Her daddy squeezed her shoulder again, guiding her to the middle seat in the first row. He nudged her to sit, following suit, plopping his hefty body into the aisle seat next to her. She was glad he didn't respond to the deformed man with the dog. Her daddy was unfiltered and would say anything that came to mind. She loved his honesty and straightforwardness. Sometimes people took him the wrong way.

"Great leg room," her daddy said, stretching his legs out.

Ezra looked it up online, she had *cynophobia*, a pathological fear of dogs.

This was her first time flying and she was terrified of being contained in the sealed, pill-shaped contraption, with metal wings, soaring thousands of feet above the earth—plus two dogs. Gulping, she couldn't remember what they called a fear of flying.

The screens hanging from the bulkhead every four rows began to show a video with Freedom Airlines soaring eagle logo. Propaganda filled the screens, with attractive flight attendants and trustworthy pilots, welcoming people in front of the historical sites most representative of America; the screen showed the Golden Gate Bridge in San Francisco, panning to a shot of waving uniformed workers in front of the Statue of Liberty in New York City. The promotional video was followed by the routine travel safety announcement.

"Good morning, welcome aboard Flight 982, leaving Las Vegas non-stop to Miami, Florida. This is Captain Morgan speaking. The weather is clear, so it should be smooth sailing. Plan on working on your tan in less than five hours. The beaches are waiting folks! If you can give our in-flight service director your full attention, they will now lead the safety announcement."

"Ladies and gentlemen...boys and girls...and everyone else!" The animated voice of the male flight attendant resonated over the intercom. "Please follow along with our lovely flight attendant, Carmen, for the safety presentation. You can also find this information in the instruction card in the seat pocket in front of you."

Carmen stood next to Ezra's daddy's seat while she presented the safety demonstration. Ezra could smell the woman's jasmine perfume. Ezra ogled the lady's legs; they were shiny, tan, and smooth. On her petite frame, Carmen wore a navy blue, knee-length skirt, a white-collared, short-sleeve shirt and a navy sweater vest hugging her curvaceous figure. Ezra admired the woman's thin, muscular arms. Maybe, Ezra thought, someday she could be strong. She hoped.

The flight attendant's skin glowed from the Miami humidity, fruity lotions, and plenty of sunshine. She wore a glistening, dainty gold watch on one arm and two gold bangles on the other. Ezra watched the bangles slide up and down her smooth arms, as she handled the demonstration materials, beginning with the life jacket.

"A life jacket is located under your seat. To put it on,

place it over your head." Carmen pulled the demo version over her head, clipping on the waistband belt; she pulled it tight as instructed.

"Please do not inflate it while you are still inside the aircraft."

Carmen pointed to the exit rows.

"An evacuation slide and life raft are at each door."

"In case of emergency, oxygen masks will drop down in front of you. Please pull the mask down towards your face, then place the mask over your mouth and nose."

She watched Carmen's French manicured nails open and close the snap on the demonstration seatbelt, completing the safety announcement.

Ezra was a nervous thirteen-year-old. When feeling anxious, she chewed her nails, forming puny, pink stubs at the end of her long thin dark fingers. When she could no longer access any bits of nail, she would begin pulling out her kinky black hair one strand at a time to ease her nerves. She looked it up online, she had *trichotillomania*; a disorder causing her to pull her own hair out.

Ezra was born in Las Vegas.

"We moved for new opportunities," her daddy had explained about his apparent opportunity to drive a limousine in Las Vegas and move from his hometown in Melbourne, Florida.

Ezra had colic when she was born and had screamed for hours. At the same time her mother was diagnosed with postpartum depression, leaving her unable to deal with the inconsolable sick infant. Her parents were young, in a new place, with no friends or family. This forced her daddy to take care of Ezra. Her daddy Darnell was her hero.

Dressed in a black suit and tie with dark shades over his eyes, he would bring the long sleek limousine home after his shift, offering Ezra and her friends' free rides down the Las Vegas Strip. The girls would sing along with Rihanna, belting out *Live your Life*.

She knew her daddy would keep her safe from that dog. Her daddy, Darnell, was looking at her now with concern. He was watching her fidgety big brown eyes nervously looking back at the dogs behind her.

"Did ya know my family had a dog when I was a li'l boy?" Darnell asked Ezra.

She looked over at him all relaxed in the seat next to her. He was leaned back with his legs splayed outward in worn out gray sweatpants, white Nike high tops, and a black L.A. Raiders t-shirt.

She was surprised to hear he had a dog—he didn't like dogs either.

She shook her head *no*.

"Yep, his name was Moses, medium-size brown mutt. He liked all us kids, when we was playing outside. He was always bark'n and jump'n up and down from his doghouse he was tied to cross the yard. We tried to give him attention as much as we could. Throw'n him scraps after breakfast and dinner. Pops wasn't so mean to that dog, and sometimes he would even talk to him like he was a person when he come home from work."

"He would say, 'Moses you chase off them scumbags today?'" Her daddy smiled. "Then pops would tell him he was a good guard dog."

"Did you touch the dog?" Ezra asked him, her dark eyes opened wide.

"Like I say, Moses was more of guard dog, we touched him plenty when we would feed him. We liked to just pat him on the head, with him rubbin' his filthy body hard against our skinny selves...taken in what he could."

The story was taking her mind off the big dog and the irritable little dog seated behind her. It was taking her mind off the high-pitched whining airplane engine.

She was curious about her daddy's dog.

"What happened to Moses?"

"Oh, it didn't end so well for the mutt. Not that any dog deserves what happened to Moses. My sister, your aunt Evette...who we're gonna see in Miami...was thinking it was time someone give Moses a bath. She took it upon herself to bring him around the front of the house and tie him off to the parked car, so she could reach the hose. She scrubbed him good and shiny. Talk'n to him sweet the whole time. She said she even dug out the crusty boogers stuck in his eyes. She loved that dog the only way she know how.

You know how eight-year-olds is, so she ran off and got distracted, leave'n Moses to dry after his bath in that humid Florida air. Mimi needed to run to the store to buy cigarettes. She sat on the velvet driver's seat of that old faded blue Buick, lit up her last smoke, pulled the shifter to R and reversed out of the driveway. The dog tied to the passenger rear bumper stumbled along the side of the vehicle, running the neighborhood streets, before reaching US 1. Then she flicked the blinker left, flicked her cigarette out the window, and accelerated to forty-five-miles-per hour. Mimi started hearing the cars honking and seeing the people waving frantically from their rolled down windows. This of course made her all the more nervous."

"Eventually, she slowed down and looked in her rear-view mirrors; everything looked fine from the left mirror, then she glanced in the right rear mirror to see the limp dog dragg'n behind her."

"Daddy what did Mimi do...was Moses dead?" Ezra's

big eyes were filled with tears from the visual of this poor animal's ordeal, even if it was a dog.

"Nearly dead. Moses was far-gone. I won't get into the gory details. She got him to the vet and put him out of his misery."

They both heard the plane speaker crackle to life. Daddy had distracted her. Ezra hadn't even noticed they were in the air.

"This is your captain speaking. We have reached a cruising altitude of 32,000 feet and I have turned off the seatbelt signs. Please feel free to get up and walk around the cabin. Thanks again for choosing Freedom Airlines and we hope you enjoy the rest of the flight."

THE SENATOR RECLINED the third-row leather first-class seat. He chose the aisle to make himself more available to the enthusiastic world traveler, Derek Beeman, who sat one seat diagonally behind him in row 4D.

His assistant, Stacy was scrolling her iPhone, leaned against the window, next to him. Her long legs were crossed and the top button on her blue and white striped shirt had popped open, exposing the top of her tanned cleavage. The senator hardly noticed the near forty-year-old Stacy. She never bothered him, quietly getting things done.

He was more interested in Derek; aware the enthusiastic Australian was cozying up to him at the bar. At this point he was curious about what Derek had planned to gain by this budding friendship with a Florida senator—he was suspicious of what the Aussie might want. A better question was, what could he gain from Derek? The senator smirked causing the scar on his cheek to stretch upward to form a thin Gamakatsu fishing hook snagging his face.

The senator tightened his lips, thinking back to the hefty weight of the impressive Pitbull, as it shook the plane on boarding. He had watched it carefully amble ahead of an elderly lady, her muumuu covered in red poinsettias, leading her in a parade like a queen. She wobbled precariously, leaning on a cane with a silver elephant for a handle. The dog had locked its luminous amber eyes with the senator for a split second, showing no sign of interest before trudging past.

He reached up and touched the thin line, running diagonally from his cheek to his lip. People told him it was hardly noticeable. He put foundation on the scar to conceal it from questions and stares—as well as his own vanity—only letting his guard down with his family.

"It looks like Captain Hook's hook," his daughters would tease him about looking the part of the villain in their favorite story.

"Watch out!" He would run after the squealing girls. "It's going to hook you with kisses!"

Sitting in his cushy seat, with a drink in hand, the senator prepared his thoughts for an upcoming debate with a democratic opponent. He needed to show the appearance of goodwill and accommodation to both his voters and wealthy donors. Recently, he had voted for a federal court judge, who had been highly undesirable on the left. The new conservative justice was strongly anti-abortion, making this a monumental victory for the Republican Party. The senator was tenacious in his anti-abortion stance and voiced this objective to the conservative Palm Beach district. He had been given no choice but to vote for the disliked judge, or the voice of his constituents would be heard in the ballot box come November. He had angry liberal Florida voters, outside vocal feminists, and activists in favor of women's healthcare, infiltrating his offices, demanding answers to his vote.

The issue making him uncomfortable was that the new judge supported ending government subsidized low-income grants that helped pay for women's healthcare. The senator had recognized the need for affordable healthcare after visiting an alternative school in Brevard County. The school was attempting to set up a daycare facility that would help young mother students wanting to complete their education. He respected these young black and Latino women for choosing to take the difficult road; raising a child while still being adolescents themselves. The girls had surrounded him, explaining that if they were able to obtain free birth control, they would promise to use it.

"They're always asking for a handout," the senator told a pompous congressman, while sitting on the passenger side of the golf cart. "It sounded almost like they were threatening me...with babies and abortions, that is."

Then the idea slammed him like a golf ball to the noggin; if young women could prevent pregnancy—then they could also prevent abortions. The senator hated abortion, and most of the people he socialized with also condemned it. All agreeing it would be best for poor people to stop reproducing.

"Certainly, you don't want these poor colored people, making more brown babies," he had asked the same pompous congressman, as the man took his shot for par on the eighth hole.

The senator adamantly claimed to be the least racist person he knew. He was well aware of what was right and wrong, having grown up the son of a Florida judge.

"Everyone knows there is a difference between *them*,"

his judge father repeatedly told him when he was growing up. "Son, you remember now...a nigg-a is your friend...and a nigg-er I put in prison."

The senator voiced his brilliant idea to provide poor women with government-subsidized birth control to a group of deciders at the country club. The men sat in wingback, forest-green leather chairs, in a warmly lit cigar room. Tobacco smoke created a dreamy blue filter throughout the space. Two thick wooden doors, beautifully carved with palm trees, separated the smoking room from the elegant mahogany bar. The ballroom-sized area was adorned with chandeliers, twinkling in the afternoon light. The warm glow came from the goliath windows that faced out onto the lakes, dotting the golf course beyond.

The response was not what he had been hoping for.

"We need to make it clear, this idea of free birth control is not an option," the governor responded to the senator's appeal.

"I have research backing me up."

The senator pulled out a manila envelope. It held printed documents, organized by color-coded paper clips. "Look here, this graph shows how fifty percent of abortions could be prevented if women had access to affordable care."

"Mike, we do not think giving away American taxpayers money is the way to end baby killings," said a Florida congressman leaning back in a huff. "We finally have the opportunity to end abortion for good. Why the hell would we take halfway on this issue, when we can have the whole Goddamn thing?"

"Think of the Medicaid, food stamps, and housing costs the taxpayer could save if all these poor people stopped having all those babies," Mike responded to the congressman.

Another deep-pocketed billionaire, superstore titan, and big donor cleared his throat, and then he took several puffs from his cigar.

"It would be in your best interest to keep your thoughts to yourself from now on Mike. I'm not paying for some floozy to fuck for free."

The senator slunk back into his chair and didn't speak the rest of the afternoon.

"Maybe these boss guys aren't so pro-life after all," he had whined to his wife after the meeting.

"It's a dog-eat-dog world Mike."

She never coddled him.

The church didn't form his ideology, science did. He had read that the chance of being born was ten followed by 2,640,000 zeroes; less chance of being born than all the atoms in the universe.

"It's a miracle of science," he mumbled the enigma to himself.

The senator always liked science, following the numbers, statistics, and facts. He had thrown these ideologies away to pander to his audience. His convictions no longer mattered.

He knew saving the environment was a lost cause at this point. All the coral reefs and large animals would be gone in the next twenty years. One hundred corporations produced most of the carbon emissions in the world. Those corporations weren't going anywhere; a single-family recycling plastic water bottles to help the environment was laughable. Miami was already under water.

"We are having the Florida government stop using the unsubstantiated claims of *global warming* and *climate change,* along with the word *sustainable,*" the Florida Governor had informed the senator and several colleagues after a fundraising luncheon. "The misdirecting words will be removed from any government communications or reports."

"Hey Mike, are you sleeping?" He heard Derek ask from one row back.

When the senator turned to face Derek, he found the man was holding a mixed drink in his hand, displaying a politician's grin.

"So, what were you doing in Vegas?" Derek queried, stirring his drink with the plastic straw.

"I had a meeting with an investment group. They have expressed interest in helping grow the Florida economy." The senator shot a wide-tooth grin back to Derek, spewing the same bullshit rhetoric he always did. "It could mean more jobs and better pay for hundreds of Floridians."

Derek feigned interest, nodding his head with vigor.

"What would this group be investing in, Senator?"

The politician responded with a one-word answer.

"Energy."

The senator took a moment to contemplate the future of his home state. After agreeing to work with the investment group on the energy deal, he envisioned the apocalyptic postcard scene; beachgoers pointing at hundreds of black rigs, pumping oil in front of the spectacular tangerine and peach sun as it set over the Gulf of Mexico coastline.

"It sounds intriguing," Derek said. "Anything to help with the economy, right?

The first-class flight attendant, a middle age woman, with faded auburn hair twisted into a bun, approached him and introduced herself as Nancy. The senator didn't care.

"Would you like the chicken cordon bleu or the beef Wellington, Senator Young?"

The senator was still feeling satiated from the chicken wings he had eaten at the airport bar.

"I'm not hungry—bring me another martini—extra dirty this time."

"Do you like speedboats, Senator?" Derek asked as soon as the flight attendant returned to the galley. "After we land I'm planning on doing some extreme sightseeing. The plan is to cruise the speedboat used in the original Miami Vice television program that starred Don Johnson."

Derek's big hands motioned energetically, as he described the power held by the captain of these agents of speed.

"Senator you should really try it," Derek encouraged him. "That is—being captain of a speedboat."

"I have the afternoon free, right Stacy?" The senator asked his assistant.

"By the way," Derek queried the senator. "Have you heard about the manatee conservation group with the FWC?"

THE FOOD CART had already clanked passed his row. He waved away the cracker and cheese gourmet snack kit the flight attendant had offered. He always said no to foods containing carbohydrates or dairy. Sitting across the aisle from him, he noticed the ponytailed, crooked-faced guy, had also passed on the snack pack. Nick assumed the man couldn't eat crackers, because he was missing the right side of his jawbone.

Nick was waiting impatiently for the drink cart to pass. He frequently darted his head into the aisle to see if it had progressed. The man next to him did the same. Nick was craving a V8 juice. Planning to mix it with a packet of *On the Go Green Juice Protocol* to supply the optimum electrolyte-vitamin punch needed on this germ-infested flight. Nick reached above his head to twist the air pressure knob and stop any re-circulated air from blowing directly on him. He admired his defined bicep as he twisted the dial shut. Looking back at his phone the screen showing black from looking away temporarily. Seeing his reflection on the face, he smoothed the top of his red hair back in one sweeping motion before swiping the screen to glow bright again.

He had just finished working the week-long Las Vegas Health Expo. It seemed an oxymoron; having a health expo in a seedy city like Vegas. It was a city that never sleeps—rampant with drugs, alcohol and prostitution. The dogma of Sin City conflicted with Nick's own healthy Christian values.

This weekend he had a mission to sell as much of the *Green Juice Protocol* to as many vendors as possible. He realized quickly the last thing people wanted to talk about while high, drunk, and gambling, was making healthy life choices. Reaching partyers the following morning proved easier, with people rethinking their previous night's poor decisions.

"Would you like to taste the *Green Juice Protocol* pick-me-up?" Nick would offer free samples to people walking past his booth from 8am to 8pm.

He enjoyed spreading the healthy living lifestyle. However, his dream was to live in the mountains and ride mountain bikes every day. Instead, he lived on a concrete slab metropolis, Los Angeles, California, so he could be near the *Green Juice Protocol* company headquarters. He had earned gold-level status as a salesperson for the multi-level marketing company.

Sweating to Kings of Leon, U2, Lifehouse, and a mix of other Christian bands, he would push the pedals of his carbon-composite frame, full-suspension mountain bike, propped on a stationary bike stand that faced a white wall in the guest/workout room of his apartment. Exercise was how he maintained his perfect physique and how he released the pent-up frustrations from the demands of maintaining the L.A. lifestyle.

He wouldn't be mountain biking while in Miami. The only rise in elevation was the foul-smelling Mount Trashmore: a two-hundred-and-eighty-foot mountain of trash looming over the south Florida Turnpike.

Nick understood the importance of keeping up his health regimen when he was traveling by airplane. This morning, like every morning, he began with a strict checklist of vitamins and mineral supplements; in the correct ratio to the food menu plan he had personally designed for optimum energy retention and muscle building proteins.

"My body is a temple," Nick would tell people, as he peered down to admire his flexed arm muscles. "A gift from God can only be treated with total consciousness."

This regimen started with the list of vitamins A-Z: vitamin A for healthy eyes, B for energy production, vitamin C for skin elasticity, consumed with his daily fruit.

"Cantaloupe should never be eaten after ANYTHING else or it putrefies in the gut, causing slowdown in digestion, and discomfort," he would enthusiastically expel the information onto his clients. "I only eat it in the morning on an empty stomach."

Vitamin D for strong bones, E for blood circulation, K from the kale and spinach in his fiber filled shake, along with calcium and magnesium supplements to help with sleep and depression. He limited dairy, because of lactose intolerance, instead enjoying a high protein diet, full of high-grade, grass-fed, pasture-raised meats, providing plenty of iron.

Nick had already prepared a week's worth of meals, each individually packed into reusable plastic Tupperware, labeled with the date; grilled chicken, broccoli, salad with a lemon wedge, little snack pouches, hard boiled eggs, and nuts packaged for easy grab and go snacks.

Growing up, Nick's parents fed him mostly sugar filled packaged foods. He tried to hold back the resentment he felt towards them for making him suffer as a fat redheaded adolescent. He was made aware of his appearance by the school kids merciless taunts that "gingers would take over the world," and "What's the difference between a shoe and a ginger...a shoe has a soul!"

When he was a teenager, the bullies dubbed him "fire crotch." After a long day of endless torment, his pock-marked face turned bright red, and with a cracking voice he screamed back at the aggressors, "My pubic hairs are black...not red!"

Then Nick, his neck and face flush from the heat of the moment, pulled down the elastic waistband of sweatpants, flashing the taunting teens his fuzzy black-haired balls. They laughed. Then they reported him to the office. He was expelled that same day. Having just turned eighteen, the police charged Nick with public lewdness against minors. He was assigned community service and the sexual charge was placed on his permanent record.

He would return home after cleaning the community center's bathrooms; penance for his actions. In desperate need of comfort foods, he would gorge on processed junk. His chunky fingers gripping the spoon, as he breathed heavily over numerous bowls of Fruity Pebbles, chomping down snack cakes, and guzzling liters of Mountain Dew. Watching reruns of *Jerry Springer, Master Chef* and *Judge Judy* to numb his mind from the daily persecution by his peers.

After "the incident," Nick found himself at a nadir of lows. He was looking for something or someone to believe in —for a community. Scrolling Facebook with only thirteen friends, half of whom were family, he discovered Drew

Rizzo. He was a health food prophet and online infomercial guru for *Green Juice Protocol*. The man was truly electrifying—inspirational. Nick emailed, inquiring on how he might join the health conversation.

Dear Drew Rizzo,

I have watched your YouTube videos and want to be part of something as amazing as the 'Green Juice Protocol' project. Sometimes I feel like I can't get out of bed, I'm so tired and overweight, ugly with pimples, and my hair is thinning. I feel so rejected. I'm always the underdog, Drew. What can I do to make the first step in becoming more like you?

Yours truly,
Nick Samson

He responded personally.

Dear Nick,

We are going to make you feel good again, with your promise and dedication to the 'Green Juice Protocol' lifestyle. We will have you on the right track in no time. I would like for you to purchase a case of the green drink, to take the first step towards a new invigorating lifestyle. You will feel more energy, with radiant glowing skin, and weight loss in your future. If you look good you feel good!

P.S. Have you thought about getting a dog? Or you could join a local therapy group, or church, to meet people in the community and talk about these problems.

Namaste,
Drew Rizzo

Nick went out the same day he received the return corre-spondence and put down a deposit on a beautiful fawn boxer puppy; she had a white chest and little white mitten paws. He named her Lola. The following day Nick joined the Los Angeles Christ First Church.

———

A stocky silver dog was sitting several rows behind Nick, on the other side of the aisle. He had first observed the dog in the airport terminal, as it sashayed past him to join the queue to board. It had the same smooshed, dark velvet snout as Lola. White fur began at its chin, running down the inside of its neck and chest. The *pit* also had white paws like his Lola, but he was silver and about sixty pounds heavier.

Glancing back over his shoulder for another look, Nick could see the dog observing the cabin intently. As the dog studied the tight enclosure, its amber gaze locked with Nick's.

Teeth.

The service dog revealed its pointed pearl whites smiling from ear to ear. It was the same contagious grin as Lola's.

Nick darted his eyes several times to dissect the misshapen face of the man sitting in his row, across the aisle.

"Hi der," the ponytailed man caught him red handed staring at his face deformity.

"Uh...hi," Nick awkwardly looked away.

"What awe you ooing in Miami?" The man asked Nick.

Nick couldn't understand him through his slurred speech. He hoped the man didn't just say, "What are you looking at?"

"Excuse me?" Nick asked.

The man repeated the question. Nick answered with a question.

"Have you heard of the *Green Juice Protocol*? It's changed my life. My name is Nick...and you are?"

"I'm Max," the man answered with a half grin. "I'm always intewested in hearing about heawthy alternatives."

CAN'T TEACH AN OLD DOG NEW TRICKS

IT was several hours into the flight, and Aunt June was still feeling anxious over the messy haired woman who sat across the aisle from her and Buster, before being escorted from the airplane for having a dog allergy. Aunt June felt guilty having the dog on the airplane. She and Buster should have had to wait, instead.

"When did dogs become more important than people?" Her voice quivered, speaking to Buster. She continuously patted him on the neck with her wrinkled hand.

She was glad Buster wasn't flying in the cargo hold with the other dogs. She had read a story recently about a Jagdterrier chewing its way out of its cage in the cargo hold and then breaking into the cages of several other dogs and killing the animals while their owners sat above. It was overwhelming for her to think of the fear those poor dogs must have felt trapped in a tight space with such a ferocious animal. And then she read that the owners claimed the dog to be the "nicest dog in the world."

Now the allergic young lady's seat across the aisle from her sat empty. A blond woman was sitting next to the window in the row in front of the empty seat. Aunt June hadn't seen the lady move an inch in the last two hours. She must be a deep sleeper.

Aunt June cocked her head to see how far the beverage cart had progressed. She was thirsty for a Diet Coke. The cart was still several rows ahead. The pretty young stewardess, Carmen, handed a V8 Juice to the muscular, redheaded man in a red shirt. Aunt June turned her head, looking towards the back of the plane, making eye contact with a tall man, his eyes shaded by a white cowboy hat. He was seated behind her on the opposite side. She smiled. He nodded his head in greeting and returned the friendly gesture.

Yip...yip...yip! The agitated little dog, two rows ahead, began barking again.

The truth was she treated Buster as good, if not better, than a human being. He fit in nicely at the trailer park. He would walk with her at a turtle's pace around one of the park loops, twice daily. The walker she used had a seat, so she could pause for a break when she became too winded. He never tugged at her, instead he waited patiently when she stopped for a rest. Buster ignored all the trailer park's barking dogs. Random strangers and park tenants were always walking up to them to make remarks about Buster.

"I got me a red-nose *pit*, but this dog takes mine to the cleaners," the nephew of a neighbor told her. "Biggest damn Blue Nose Pitbull I ever saw."

Neighborhood children would ask to pet Buster. They really weren't supposed to, because Buster was a service dog. Cindy had cautioned her against letting strangers approach the working animal.

Aunt June could tell that children were the dog's weakness. He loved them. When a child would approach, he could hardly maintain his cool working dog demeanor. The big dog would start to fidget his feet; tap dancing back and forth with his white paws clicking. Thrilled for the opportunity to touch, to smell, and to taste them. She again wondered about his life before Cindy had adopted him from the shelter.

He had terrible dreams, and would let out small whimpers, as he kicked and pawed at the empty air. Buster's upper lip would pull back into a twitching snarl, snapping his menacing fangs, as his legs ran from or towards something in these nap terrors. She had Buster take Wilbur's spot on the bed next to her, so she could help keep him calm when he had the bad dreams. It was comforting for her also to feel the warmth of his body against hers. At breakfast she would make double portions, passing Buster bacon and eggs from the table. They were partners.

———

Wilbur and Aunt June had had a Miniature Schnauzer named Oscar when they moved to Albuquerque. The scruffy small dog was nearly ten years old at the time and followed Wilbur everywhere.

"Oscar has the energy and the curiosity of a puppy," Wilbur used to tell her.

Wilbur had been unpacking the van after they returned from their road trip to Carlsbad Caverns in southeast New Mexico. It had become tricky traveling with the dog when they realized the state park wouldn't allow the animal into the humid underground caves. She and Wilbur had to take turns caring for Oscar, while the other person discovered stalagmites and the stalactites solo below the earth. Wilbur was exhausted from the desert heat and the long drive. He hurriedly unloaded the last of the items from the van, while June placed the leftover sandwich fixings in the refrigerator and started a load of laundry.

Wilbur went to lie down in the bedroom. June turned the television to *Wheel of Fortune* and started preparing Hamburger Helper. After they finished supper, they both sat watching *60 minutes*. When Andy Rooney concluded the program, Wilbur turned to June.

"Where's Oscar?"

"That's funny," she said. "I haven't seen him in hours."

They searched the length of the trailer and then went outside calling for him into the warm starry night.

"When was the last time you saw him?" Wilbur asked June.

"I guess this afternoon when we got back from the trip."

Getting ready for bed that night the room felt empty without Oscar. Every night he would pack down the blanket placed at the foot of the bed. The little mutt would turn in twenty circles before snuggling in between their feet.

"I'm worried about Oscar," June fretted, clicking off the bedside lamp.

They lay in the dark room side-by-side, listening to each other's lumbering breaths.

"Did you check the van?"

Wilbur shot out of bed, wearing only his boxer shorts, his hard, round gut protruded over the top of the elastic waistband. He hobbled quickly towards the van, guided by the light of a full moon.

Wilbur died, one month to the day, after he found Oscar smothered in the hot vehicle. Aunt June had kept the story a secret from Buster. She knew he could smell Wilbur and Oscar in the house. They had both been through enough, she figured.

Her nephew Kyle had purchased her the airplane ticket to Miami as a birthday gift. She had been too afraid to fly before getting Buster, and was desperate to visit her sister Angela, Kyle's mother, who was passing time in a nursing home in Fort Lauderdale. Kyle had planned to accompany her on the trip to see his mother, but the Kellogg's factory he managed developed a malfunction with the Fruit Loops machine. He was forced to cancel the trip, now having to deal with large amounts of plastic that had been ground into the brightly colored sugared flour—contaminating the batch —resulting in a recall.

Buster had been acting skittish since boarding the airplane. When the plane was getting ready for take-off the high-pitched whine of the engine made him stand alert in his seat. He began panting profusely from his open mouth. This was strange behavior for him. He was usually so calm and collected. *What would Cindy think?* She wondered. Cindy had told her he would be fine to fly. Buster seemed to regain his composure after they were at cruising altitude and even lay his head in her lap. She felt his soft even breathing against her legs, where his sizable velvet head now rested.

I CAN SMELL the stranger's fear—his pheromones penetrate my nose. I am alert to his accelerated breathing pattern. I smell the perspiration produced under his arms. He's nervous. I don't like it. Bang! Phreeeeeet! My ears begin ringing from gunshots—and the nagging whistle— gunpowder irritates my nose. I'm running outside into the sunshine, snarling, the metallic flavor of blood has filled my mouth. The gas odor from the low-rider's exhaust lingers in the air, choking my lungs. The car's engine fades away, leaving the sound of my heavy breathing, and the clicking of my nails against melting asphalt. My paws are on fire, tracking bloody prints down the roadway. I run faster.

"Buster wake up," I can hear Aunt June's soothing voice, stirring me from the recurring dream.

My one leg continued to kick softly, as she gently brushed my hackle down with her warm hands. She had already removed my service vest when I was panting earlier.

Now, my one amber eye opened cautiously to connect with her crystal blue ones, blurred behind her thick glasses.

The bright fluorescent cabin lights felt like a cat's claws scratching my eyeballs. The feeling of immense sadness had overcome me after waking from the distressing dream. It had been a long day. I must have drifted off with the drone of the plane's engine. Leaving me confused about how long we had been trapped in our seats. I was having difficulty keeping track of time.

Breath in, I told myself. *Breath out*.

"Sweet thing...you were having a bad dream."

She rubbed behind my ears. I continued to rest my head in her lap. Inhaling her scent; the familiar powdery smell comforted me from the obscene jumble of odors that enveloped the loud rumbling machine. The plastic chemical outgassing from the interior walls and the cushioned seats of the plane, was the predominant odor, making it harder to detect where the other flavors' exact locations were. Plus, Aunt June had told me to remain in my place. I wanted so badly to personally sniff every passenger and their luggage. Sitting in my seat, the fragrances were blending together, forming a perfume of confusing chaos.

Jasmine flowers filled the air. The woman who had helped us to our seats earlier was pulling the cart past. She stopped next to Aunt June.

"What can I get you to drink?"

I sat up to let Aunt June lower her tray table from the seat in front of her, turning my attention to the flight attendant, who was filling a plastic cup with ice. She popped the tab on the can of Diet Coke Aunt June had requested. I could hear it fizzing and bubbling, as she handed over. The sweetness made me want to sneeze.

Sitting upright, I took a deep drag from the cabin's

circulated air. I whiffed the little dog a few seats in front of me. I hadn't seen the dog when it boarded the plane, but I had sensed it right away. The *mini wolf* had been belting out three rapid barks in succession about every hour. I wished I could greet the tail-wagger. If I could just sniff his rear end, I'd be able to know how old he was and what he ate for breakfast. Taking a deep breath to inhale the human stink all around me, I smelled the deliciously nasty human armpit. It produces the most profound source of odor by any animal. Human genitals reek more than a dog's butthole. Their skin emits odorous fluids, oils, and sweat, giving each person a signature scent. At that moment, I could smell cancer on the man a few seats in front of me—the human master of the *mini wolf*.

When Aunt June's friends would come to visit the trailer home, I knew how many cats, dogs, and children they had. I knew what the visitor had for lunch, and what items they purchased at the grocery store to make for dinner. I knew if they washed their hands after going to the bathroom. I could smell the faint dribble of urine left in the crotch of their underwear and I knew if they suffered from disease. I like to bury my face in the space between their legs and inhale everything about them—to get to know them.

I don't have names for all the diseases, but I can tell when a person is sick.

Cindy would use big words to describe the different odors revealed during my training: epilepsy, narcolepsy, malaria, and Parkinson's disease. The scents most familiar to me were cancer and diabetes. Aunt June's disease was diabetes. My friend Cindy taught me to sit next to Aunt June and paw her leg if I detected a change in her blood sugar levels.

"You can smell odors at concentrations of parts per trillion," Cindy explained to me. "They say it's like smelling one rotten apple in two million barrels."

I loved apples.

"It means you can smell real good!" She laughed.

I was feeling constrained, sitting on my seat, trapped inside this rumbling machine. I could feel my tension building with the whine of the engine.

A little boy, my height, went running down the aisle past me. I stretched my neck to follow him, peeking over the seat behind me to watch him disappear out of site.

Pat...Pat...Pat.

His little feet were hitting the floor of the plane, as he ran back up the aisle, passing me again.

I wanted to smell more of him. I wanted my scratchy tongue to lick the boogers from his baby soft face. I love kids.

I heard him running back, *Pat...Pat...Pat.*

My white paws started to dance in my seat. *Oh boy!* He slowed as he approached Aunt June and myself.

"Is dis yawh dwag?" He pointed at me, asking Aunt June.

Cindy told me dogs could learn a vocabulary of up to one-hundred-and-fifty words. I knew many more words than she thought possible.

I recognized Aunt June was thrilled to be speaking with the tiny person. Her heart beat faster—like my own.

"Yes honey, Buster is my dog, my friend, and my helper," Aunt June told the little boy proudly.

"Can I pwet him?"

I'm about to lose control with excitement. I know I shouldn't show my immense enthusiasm—I need to act cool.

"Sure, sweet thing...put your palm out and let him sniff you first," she instructed.

His hand was reaching towards me. I could taste him in the air. He was delicious.

I have already inhaled his skin, but now with his sticky stink directly under my nose, I smell sweet candy, dirt, soap, baby diapers, Goldfish crackers, and boogers.

"He likes to be petted behind the ears," Aunt June tells the freckled face boy.

"His eaws are hawd," the little boy says, reaching behind my small-cropped ears to rub my giant bowling ball of a head.

I felt his warm, sticky fingers catching on my fur.

The nostalgia comforts me—before Aunt June and before Cindy I had human children to love—if I could only remember.

The boy held a small toy plane in his hand. He raised is up and buzzed the little plane down, making a *vroom* sound through his teeth. He smiled at Aunt June and me.

"Fanks!" He spit out, zooming his airplane away.

My glowing amber eyes watched the small boy buzz off.

Then I spotted the redheaded man across the aisle sitting stiffly. I inhaled his anxiety; the chemicals from this disorder covered his skin like a film. The man was suffering from a different kind of disease—an emotional one. He held a shiny cell phone in the palm of his hand, his fingers swiping and scrolling through the pictures, pushing heart shapes when he liked a shot. I understood him to be loving the pictures of smiling, strong people.

The boy stomped several rows up the aisle to his mother. I could see the back of her head protruding from above the seat near the window. I had smelled her on him. The sour smell of crusted breast milk. Her oily hair had penetrated his striped shirt; from her having gone days without a shower. I smelled marijuana. I smelled baby powder. I smelled the baby.

Aunt June pulled out a magazine from the pocket on the seat in front of her. It was the Freedom Magazines for the airline. Flipping through the pages, Aunt June held the pictures out in front of her, all the better to see.

I took the opportunity to view the photos she held up. She flipped the pages to uncover people in nicely lit restaurants laughing, close images of gourmet food and wine, and then we studied a page that showed an ad for a hotel with an infinity swimming pool overlooking a beachscape.

Time passed. The sound of the plane continued to grate on my nerves. Both the monotone buzz and the high-pitched jet engine penetrated deep into my eardrums, cracking my exterior composure. I started to pant again, trying to calm myself by looking out the round window on my left.

BUCKEYE's massive body encroached on the aisle way. His significant height was squeezed tightly between the economy section seats. He stood 6'4 in his size fourteen cowboy boots—his limbs were bursting out of the row. The man hunched his wide shoulders, trying to fit into the compact space, pulling his tattooed forearms onto his lap, attempting to shrink himself.

Buckeye was the US Air Marshall assigned to keep an eye on Senator Mike Young on the return flight to Miami. Recently, the senator had been receiving death threats, following a controversial vote. It was common practice to keep the in-flight assignments top secret. Buckeye was sitting in the exit row, in the middle of the economy section. Nobody on board the flight knew he was an air marshal, not even the senator.

At the ticket counter, the airline agent had given him the exit row upgrade after observing his considerable size.

"I don't think you would fit in a regular economy seat!" She had teased him.

"Yes ma'am, that sounds just fine."

He was dressed in worn down Wranglers and dusty cowboy boots. He wore a Navajo designed turquoise eagle on his silver belt buckle, a gift from his now deceased father. His faded gray t-shirt hugged his muscles, while clinching the extra ten pounds he had gained around his waist; a birthday gift for turning forty-five. Buckeye's dark kind eyes were shaded by a cream-colored Stetson cowboy hat.

It was a fine spot to be in the middle of the plane. He could just see into the first-class section, with a clear view of the senator sitting in the aisle seat along the opposite side. He would have a direct line of sight to the politician until the flight attendant closed the dividing curtain. The senator appeared to be in rapt conversation with a clean-cut, dark haired man sitting behind him.

Buckeye regarded the old lady, Aunt June, accompanied by her service dog, one seat in front of him, on the other side of the aisle. Buckeye heard the elderly woman introduce herself and the dog to the messy haired woman, who was later escorted off the plane due to an allergy to dogs. Federal law ensures access to air transportation on all carriers for all individuals with a service animal. It was an interesting switch from the normal cultural animal hierarchy—where humans rule and dogs drool.

He had had several run-ins with the Staffordshire or American Pitbull breed during his years in law enforcement. Buckeye felt it was the owner, and how the dog was raised, that determined if the dog was aggressive or not. Buster was a bit frightening to look at with his larger than normal girth and cropped ears. Stewart supposed he was judging the dog based on its appearance, like people judged him for his tattoos and towering stature. He figured the dog probably had a fine disposition, seeing as a geriatric person was in charge. However, any strange dog was an unknown risk.

He knew Pitbulls were responsible for more than half of all dog attack injuries in the United States. It was likely they got a bad rap from of the company that kept them. He visualized the stereotypical *pit* owner not as a sweet little old lady, but some skinny punk kid wearing baggy pants and a wife-beater tank top, high on tweak. After meeting the much-maligned Pitbull breed, he found they were usually friendly enough.

The owners of the animals were a different story. Statistically, they were more likely to have criminal convictions for aggressive crimes, drugs, alcohol, domestic violence, and infractions involving children and firearms. The dogs were originally bred as catch dogs for hunting and attacking large animals like wild boar. They were reared for pit fighting.

Buckeye was more of a herder dog kind of guy. He liked the border collie and Australian shepherds, but he mostly connected with the devoted shorthaired cow dog—A.K.A. ankle biter—the blue heeler.

Buckeye was raised on a cattle ranch in Southwest Colorado, through the Dolores River valley, and into the mountains along the West Fork dirt road. His family's hundred-year-old, two-story log farmhouse was in the middle of a meadow, in the middle of four hundred acres of high mountain pine and aspen forest: surrounded by freshwater streams, natural hot springs, snow fed rivers and lakes.

Next in line, his older brother decided to take over the family ranch. Stewart was left to join the military. Being a cowboy, it was easy for him to excel in the Navy: driven, athletic, tolerant, a perfect shot; he was a natural born killer.

Between deployments, while serving as a Navy SEAL,

he made his home in Thailand. Closing his eyes Stewart took in a deep breath, letting the wave of the memory surge over him. He was relaxing on a white sand beach, a short walk from his home, with his Thai girlfriend, Malee. He remembered her lying on her stomach, propped up on her elbows, barely clothed in a small, white crocheted bikini—bright against her dark skin. She was scooping handfuls of white sand, sifting it through her fingers over and over, sometimes picking out a microscopic shell to admire.

Malee had speculated in a soft accented voice, "If I were stuck on an island and had to pick one person...hmm... definitely you Stewart."

He marveled at how animals could be treated so differently based on geography. It would be outrageous to expect the United Emirates Airlines to allow a dog to travel in the cabin. He had read in the teachings of Islam that the saliva of a dog is impure, and objects that come into contact with a dog's saliva must be washed seven times. A dog flying with humans was as laughable as a pig flying first class. Everyone knows pigs can't fly. He smiled.

When he had lived in Thailand with Malee, they opted not to own a dog. The neighbors, however, a Dutch man who had married a local Thai woman, had a puppy. Buckeye noticed the dog shortly after the couple had brought it home. They would sit in the front yard with their two small children, throwing a chartreuse tennis ball for the fluffy pup. Its white shaggy mane hung in its face, shading its eyes like a sheepdog.

Months passed before he noticed the dog's incessant barking. Its fur had formed black dreadlocks from spending its short life tied to a tree stump in the yard, with only a tipped over pan for water. Then the rain started. During the monsoons, he watched the dog howling under the torrential downpour. With no shelter and only a few feet of rope tethering it to a stump.

Buckeye had sat on his front porch listening to the roar of the deluge against the metal roof and the sound of crying and barking coming from next door. He had had enough. Heading down the front steps of his home, he walked into the torrent completely drenching his t-shirt and jeans, taking large strides to the neighbor's house on his bare feet. He let loose a barrage of pounding on the front door. The tall light-haired Dutch man answered the banging nonchalantly. He seemed confused by the large American visitor.

"What is the plan with that dog?" Buckeye demanded the Dutch man, water running off his eyebrows and down his cheeks, forming freshwater tears.

The Dutch man looked perplexed, "Nothing. What do you want with Bruce?"

"I want you to untie Bruce and let him go, at least that way he can find himself some food," Buckeye kept his voice level, spitting a loogie of tobacco onto the lawn.

"I have tried," the Dutch man said. "He always comes back, then jumps on my car to get my attention—scratching it!" The Dutch man pointed to his red Mercedes parked in the driveway. Buckeye didn't see any scratches. "Do you want the dog?"

Buckeye was in a predicament—exactly as he had feared. People who put their noses in another person's business...often get a nasty whiff. Bruce had become his problem when he knocked on the Dutch man's door. If he left the dog tied to the tree it would live out a tortured existence during the monsoon season, before being saved from the relentless agony by starvation.

He had no interest in having a dog but knew a German expat woman who had helped home stray dogs before. She lived nearby in Khao Lak. He told the Dutch man he was going to look into finding the dog a better home, returning to his house to call the German woman. She agreed to help.

"Will you get the dog from your neighbor?" The woman asked him with a German accent. "Will you temporarily keep the dog while we look for candidates to home him?"

This was what he had hoped to avoid, not wanting to become attached to the dog. He asked his girlfriend Malee if they should help the animal. She was stirring fish head soup over the outdoor burner, wearing itty-bitty shorts and a bikini top.

"For sure, Stewart."

When Buckeye brought Bruce home, the German woman helped him shave the dreadlocked-darkened mats from his neglected body, leaving pink skin and bones. His beady black eyes spoke a million thanks. They decided it was best to keep Bruce in their fenced yard. The carport cover provided him with plenty of shelter.

When Buckeye went outside, Bruce would follow him thrilled for the company, playfully biting at his hands and jumping up on his legs. Buckeye knew the dog hadn't been around people, minus the months he was a puppy play toy. Bruce needed proper training. Buckeye wasn't the guy for the job.

The German woman called to let Buckeye know she had found a French expat woman expressing interest in meeting Bruce. When the two women arrived at the house, Bruce jumped at the French woman, biting down hard on the palm of her hand, penetrating the skin to leave a bloody mark.

"I'm not interested in Bruce," the French expat snapped at Buckeye.

Malee's four-year-old son wanted to know Bruce, but every time the boy went outside Bruce would jump on him, knocking him to the ground. He would bite at the child's hands, scaring him and making him cry. Soon the boy was too afraid to go outside and play. It wasn't like in the United States, where Buckeye could call Animal Control...or the Humane Society...or grab his gun.

The German expat called again to say she wouldn't be able to home Bruce and maybe Buckeye should investigate putting him down. He recognized this to be the compassionate thing to do. The vet would charge him two-hundred fifty US dollars to have the dog euthanized. Buckeye didn't have the money. Bruce's options had become limited. He didn't want to drop the dog at the landfill to fight off other stray dogs.

He shared his predicament with the small hunched over gardener, after he witnessed the man fighting off the pain-in-the-butt dog, while attempting to trim the grass and cut back the bougainvillea bushes. The stooped man said he knew someone who might be interested in the animal. The gardener returned excitedly the next day after finding a family who wanted to take Bruce.

"Sir, this family want dog, but no want for pet," the gardener explained. "Sir, they want to treat dog good. Feed dog food. Make fat. Bruce feed family, sir."

Buckeye's brows furrowed as he realized what the man was telling him.

"They want to eat Bruce," Buckeye grimaced, spitting

out the chew from behind his lower lip, dark juice splat-tering the sidewalk.

"Yes, they treat him good," the gardener smiled a tooth-less grin, ignoring Buckeye's bubbling brown spit.

Buckeye recognized that Bruce could feed a family... and then he tried to wrap his mind around the dog being a pet...and then a meal...all in one short conversation.

Buckeye figured food was food: be it a cow, pig, chicken, squirrel, cat, horse or a dog. He grew up on a ranch.

He thought about a prairie dog he had once shot for sport when he was a child.

"God damn it, Stewart," his father had reprimanded him. "You know these little guys mate for life." To teach him a lesson about killing animals for target practice, his dad had made him skin the little dog and grill it over the campfire. Then eat it. The vision never left him. Not of the twisting dead prairie dog on a stick, but instead, the memory of the tiny dog's mate. The female dog who kept poking her head out of their hole-for-a-home, searching with her beady black eyes for her missing partner. All the while Stewart was turning its little body over the fire's flames.

The Thai family came in a blue minivan and picked Bruce up later that day. That was the year before the Tsunami wiped out Khao Lak; in the end the little mutt Bruce would have died anyway...everyone else did.

Buckeye was tugged from his thoughts as he watched the massive dog carefully pull itself up in the seat, cocking its head to look out the window. Several seats ahead of the dog, he observed a robust redheaded man bobbing his head into the aisle, apparently, he was thirsty and willing the beverage cart to move faster. The impatient man was dressed in khaki pants and short-sleeve, red polo shirt. Buckeye had seen a logo for *Green Juice Protocol* on the right breast pocket when the man had passed him to use the toilet earlier in the flight. His muscles bulged from the hems of the too tight sleeves. Buckeye noticed the way he had held back his shoulders over confidently—puffing out his chest—overcompensating.

The snack cart bumped against Buckeye's leg, jarring his left arm. He was able to keep a firm grip on the Coke can held in his sizable hand. The can was for spitting the chewing tobacco fluids into.

He noticed the middle-aged couple sitting five rows up. They had boarded toting a small dog in a hard carrier. He had heard the little dog let out a shrill *yip* several times during the flight. Now he watched its owner, a salt and peppered ponytailed man, dressed in white paint splattered carpenter jeans, stand in the aisle to reach for a bag he had stored in the compartment above his seat. Buckeye admired the man's white t-shirt, showing a print of a tarpon jumping in front of a sunset across his back. The man shifted his stance to reveal his half missing, disfigured face. Thereupon, Buckeye spit the remaining tobacco chew from under his bottom lip into the coke can he gripped in his hand. The tin cracked under his finger pressure. The missing jawbone was a tell-tale sign the man had been a tobacco user. Buckeye had lost his appetite for leaf—at least for the moment.

A gorgeous flight attendant, Carmen was on her nametag, walked past him with her heeled shoes tapping against the carpeted floorboards. He couldn't help but admire her defined tan calf muscles.

He returned his attention to the big dog. It had started

panting. He wondered if having two dogs in such close proximity was a good idea?

The first-class flight attendant closed the curtain separating the sections, ending his line of sight to the senator. Buckeye tilted his head back and shut his eyes.

Max looked down at his ridiculously fuzzy Pomeranian. The spoiled dog, Bruno, sat in the small dog carrier between Maxine and himself. The little dog was exceptionally poufy from his wife Maxine obsessively brushing its long yellow fur. The hair formed

yellow sunbursts, popping through the holes of the carrier from all directions.

His wife spoke endearingly to Bruno in her singsong baby talk.

"Brunny baby, soft little bunny, bunny, Brunny boy," her pretty pink lips smacked kisses at the kennel. "Did Bunny see the big scary dog? Don't be scared, mama has you."

Max observed his surroundings, embarrassed that someone might hear her ridiculousness. Then he noticed the big dog that was sitting a couple of rows behind them that Maxine had been alluding to. The big dog smiled at him from ear to ear, its tongue resting between its teeth.

"I feel bad that Bruno scared that teenage girl," Max said, referring to when they had boarded the plane. "She was behind me and Bruno *yipped* at her. I thought she was going to have a heart attack!"

"That's foolish," Maxine said. "The girl's father should bring her around dogs more often. Brunny wouldn't hurt a fly."

She baby-talked to the pooch, kissing at his cage.

"No Brunny you wouldn't, would you baby?" Turning back to Max she said, "Plus he's tiny and in a cage for good- ness sakes."

Maxine and Max had been some of the last passengers to board the flight to Miami. Behind them, the final two passengers to board the aircraft were a rumpled looking, beefy black man and his rail thin teenage daughter. It was when he was trying to find their assigned seats that Bruno terrified the girl by barking aggressively at her. Max could see the father and his daughter were now sitting in the front row of the coach section.

His mind kept returning to the start of the flight.

"And, remember how that messy haired woman pointed to Bruno because she had an allergy?" Max was feeling frus- trated traveling with the little dog. "And then she was removed from the airplane!"

"The dog is an emotional support animal..." He prodded Maxine for confirmation.

Then Max locked eyes with the redheaded man in the red shirt sitting across the aisle, he explained, "We have the paperwork to back it up."

The paperwork actually assigned Max the emotional support dog, however, he felt he was mentally grounded at this point in his life. It was his wife Maxine who suffered from Post Traumatic Stress Disorder from Max being diag- nosed with stage-four squamous cell carcinoma. The cancer had originated on his tongue.

His entire life as he had known it had come to a screeching halt one Saturday morning, the year before. He was washing his fifteen-year-old, white Chevrolet pickup truck, using the power washer in the sun-drenched front driveway of his Florida home, when his cell phone rang. His world became the slow-motion option on his iPhone. He watched his wife Maxine walking towards him, with the phone to her ear. Her electric blue, gingham dress fluttered around her, turning her into a small hovering blue bird, flitting in front of him, darting about to not make eye contact. He inhaled her soft wispy fine hair, smelling of Johnson's Baby shampoo.

"It's the doctor, Max," she whispered into his chest after handing him the phone.

Damned if the doctor wasn't calling on a Saturday.

"It isn't fair!" she chirped to him after the doctor had given the devastating news.

"Life is not fair Maxine," he replied, holding her tight in his strong arms.

He had never smoked cigarettes or chewed tobacco. The doctors thought he could have the HPV virus, a major cause of cervical and oral cancers, but he tested negative.

A few days later he lay naked under a warmed white blanket, vulnerable and shaved, with a catheter up his dick. Several faceless masked nurses, each with nametags claiming the same name *Melissa*, wheeled him to surgery. The doctors were set to remove his lower right jaw and three quarters of his tongue. While he slept, they took the muscle from his chest, threading it through his neck, and into his mouth to fill the empty pocket.

"The pectoral muscle is now partially filling the empty place where the jaw once was," the surgeon had explained.

Max had zero sensation in the newly filled space in his mouth, nor could he feel what was left with his mostly absent tongue. This was a good thing, because the hair from his chest was now like the baleen of a whale, filling the inside of his right cheek.

The radiologist made a Darth Vader face mold to fit his head, bolting him to a hard bed to keep him perfectly still while they radiated his absent jaw. Later he lost most of his remaining upper teeth. After being radiated he would walk across the hallway to the oncology department; a gymnasium size hospital room, with an assembly line of cancer patients lined up in leather recliners. The sickly people were connected to IV's pumping chemo poison into the ports, surgically installed in each of their chests. The cancer patients were warmed with crafty, handmade patchwork quilts and knitted caps, donated by the Lutheran Quilting Club.

Maxine reached out to a high school friend, who had married a marijuana grower when it was still illegal in Colorado. The friends had made a good living with the illegal drug, but with it becoming a legalized medicine, the competition had become fierce and new regulations proved too strict for the old hippie. Maxine's friends continued growing marijuana, but now focused their attention on processing Rick Simpson Oil.

"RSO is made from the whole cannabis indica plant," the marijuana farmer Olli had explained over the phone. "It contains lots of both THC and CBD, great for cancer patients and general health maintenance. Studies have shown the oil can help one-year survival rates by up to thirty-percent."

Max began taking the (illegal in Florida) black tar-like liquid.

"Mix it with warm coconut oil to dilute it," Olli suggested. "Then Maxine can inject the warm medicine into the feeding tube in your stomach."

"Max you need to avoid using the doctor prescribed morphine and oxycontin," Olli told him. "It's highly addictive. And with the RSO you won't need it and you won't get sick to your stomach."

Max was given a prognosis of three to five years life expectancy. He was on a deadline. Literally. But, with the cancer diagnosis came a gift; Max now lived in the present and planned for Maxine's future.

Like his partial tongue's unfamiliarity with his mouth, Max no longer recognized the Florida he grew up in. He was a builder by trade. He couldn't help feeling guilty for his participation in covering the wetlands with drainage ditches and canals, replacing the green preserves with concrete strip malls and suburban housing developments, claiming conventional names like *Lakeside Vista,* entangled with *Pelican Estates.*

He understood it would no longer be sustainable to continue living in the Florida Keys, after their home on Grassy Key had been severely damaged in the last hurricane. The surge completely tore through their older 1940's ground level Keys home, taking all their belongings out to the ocean. The beautiful hardwood walls had been destroyed and the hand crank panel windows swept away. He could rebuild, but he was a smart enough man to know the oceans were rising, and the hurricanes would return with increased ferocity each coming year. The new weather patterns were obviously not his problem anymore, with death knocking at his washed away door. The problem was his *little bird* Maxine would be left behind.

"I'm not leaving you in a dilapidated house, centered in the bull's eye of the next hurricane," he told her.

After researching climate change, he gained a clearer understanding of the ravaging effects the new weather changes would have on the coastal communities. The Florida Keys and Miami would become submerged after being relentlessly pummeled by stronger and more intense storms each year. The south Florida population explosion would add to the pain caused by the loss of homes from the storm surges, diseases from unsanitary conditions, and lack of food to supply the humanitarian crisis.

"Where will climate scientist head with their families?" Maxine had asked.

It might have been the *little bird's* more brilliant moments.

Scientists were heading north to the cooler Scandinavian countries. The overall weather change could have positive impacts on the northern climates; with longer growing seasons and a more comfortable living environment. Although, the rising temperatures would release large amounts of carbon from the permafrost ground cover. An increase in forest fires and deadly insects would also be something to be concerned about.

Max flew Maxine north to Alaska. Because it was in the United States, it would be easier to relocate to, unlike Canada and Norway, with visa requirements proving too strict for a simple carpenter and his artist wife. In the spring they traveled to Fairbanks to scout out the terrain. The Alaskans avoided the term "spring," instead renaming the season "break up." Floating miniature icebergs jammed the colossal size puddles engulfing the parking lots.

Maxine had wrapped herself in a blue down parka and stood in Xtratuf rubber boots in a foot of water. On her head she wore a red knit hat with a rainbow pom-pom. She wasn't smiling. Her cold nose was shining red like Rudolph the reindeer. In her shivering arms she was holding Bruno. The dog's mud drenched fur stuck to its teeny quivering form.

"I'm not moving here. I'd rather die in a hurricane. And neither is Brunny."

Max started scouting out more temperate areas. He wanted to stay away from coastal locations. He wanted to stay away from large population centers. He needed a place that provided long growing seasons and substantial wild animals for food.

Maxine, Max and Bruno flew into Vegas, rented a car and began exploring the surrounding smaller Nevada and Utah communities.

Maxine agreed Castle Valley, Utah, was her favorite place they visited while traveling the western states. It was in the desert foothills of the La Sal Mountain range. Red sandcastles towered over spectacular windblown arches and canyonland vistas. It was centered among national parks, Utah state parks and BLM land. After that it was encompassed by endless desert. The nearest cities were either four hours north by car to Salt Lake City, or six hours northeast to Denver, with the Colorado River acting as a moat, separating the fertile land from the hordes of people who would later attempt to escape from the cities. It was six hours south to Albuquerque or six hours west to Las Vegas; both were separated by the endless yellow sand buttes of the Navajo and Ute reservations.

Luckily for Max, the value of their property in the Florida Keys was exorbitant, making it easy for them to afford the three-acre, four-hundred-thousand-dollar property they had purchased in Castle Valley.

"How much longer do you suppose insurance companies will find it financially feasible to keep paying out for new Florida beach houses?" He asked Maxine after receiving the insurance settlement.

"Make sure we don't forget the baby food mill," he reminded Maxine about packing for the move. "So I can still eat after the electricity goes out."

Maxine placed her knitting paraphernalia in the middle seat pocket in front of Bruno and was staring out the window at the green waters of the Gulf of Mexico below to focus on the millions of crescent shaped white caps rippling in the endless ocean water.

She sighed.

"I don't much feel like finishing the llama wool doggy sweater for Bruno."

THE LAST THING Maxine wanted to think about was packing the baby food mill. She quietly listened to Max's wild apocalyptic doomsday tirades. She followed along on his insane prepper's journey. She didn't understand why prepping mattered so much to him, if he wasn't going to be around for the end of the world anyway.

Maxine looked at the clear plastic cup, and the two empty mini bottles of white wine, dry on the tray table in front of her. Keeping her hands busy, she was knitting a sweater for Bruno.

Maxine was an artist. Her life's work was seeking out beauty and then recreating it. Her preferred art form was acrylic nature scenes; painting oceans, lighthouses, bridges, islands, trees, shells, birds, and fish swimming through the mangroves, and older, stilted shiplap island homes with brightly colored hibiscus and bougainvillea flowers. Maxine had constrained herself to paint only realistic nature scenes in perfect symmetry. She loved to paint close-ups of great herons, pelicans, and osprey. One side of the bird's face would line up in mirror form to the other side of its face—nature's harmony.

"It is scientifically proven that both animals and people are more attracted to faces with balanced profiles," her art coach explained.

She wondered if she needed to change her art to represent a more abstract Picasso-like Cubist style, now that Max's once handsome face had been mangled. It seemed the whole world appeared distorted to her now. Trees that once stood stable and firm appeared weak and hunched over; desiccated and disfigured by the dark green vine tendrils grabbing them from below.

What had once made her giddy with excitement now bored her. When the manatees came to visit in the canal behind their Keys home, she stopped feeding them the tasty lettuce and fresh water from the hose. Ignoring the gentle giants. Staring blankly at a white canvas.

Life seemed awry—off balance. Yet she felt more alive than ever. Awakening to the concreteness of an inescapable death hadn't made her happy—it made her aware.

Maybe I feel more alive because my Max is deader, she thought.

Bruno noticed Max had cancer before anyone else did. Max would lean in for a kiss from Brunny, and the little dog would back up, repulsed by his rank death breath. The pooch's miniature body of yellow fur would begin to quiver as he squatted to tinkle over the tile floor.

After the cancer was removed, Bruno stopped sprinkling the floor. While Max was recovering from chemotherapy the little dog slept between his feet, reclined high on the Lazy Boy chair with the football game playing in the background. Maxine would find Bruno licking at Max's feeding tube while he slept. Not wanting to wake Max, or to scold Bruno, she would let him lap away at the connection.

"Dogs mouths are cleaner than humans...right Brunny?"

Maxine knew she had signed on through sickness and health when they had married, she just hadn't anticipated him losing half of his mouth. Now he stumbled over his words with garbled slurs and ate pureed food.

"He is such a survivor," friends would comment. "He is the greatest guy and so strong for your family."

He used to be strong. She wept alone.

She pictured his once defined brawny build, rightfully earned from his backbreaking labor as a building contractor.

Maxine was a passionate woman. She dreamed of kissing. She would wake with her soft mouth open, still wet from the sensation of Max's lips, only moments before hard against her own—his taste lingering on her tongue. A knot would form in her throat from the overwhelming desire for the impossible—she didn't want to open her eyes. In the middle of the night she would suffer panic attacks. Waking to the pitch-black darkness, sure she had died. Going to bed was like sleeping in her tomb.

She was an artist who lost her paintings to a hurricane: her art, her passion, and her enthusiasm, washed away with the tide of apathy.

"Maxie, get me another wee bottle of white wine when the beverage cart passes pretty please," she drawled to her husband. "I'm feeling a bit peckish; how about the cheese and cracker snack pack too."

A WOLF IN SHEEP'S CLOTHING

MY MOUTH SALIVATES from puncturing the man's skin. I swallow his blood like a warm drink down my throat, the rest of the hot liquid mixes with the saliva drooling from each side of my wide mouth. Shaking my head, I whip the foaming pink strands to circle my velvet snout, forming a bloody muzzle.

"Ladies and gentlemen, this is Captain Morgan speaking, if you look out your window you will see we are currently flying above the Gulf of Mexico. We are scheduled to land in Miami in just under one hour from now. Your flight attendants will be coming through the cabin with the final beverage service. Enjoy the rest of the flight."

I smell jasmine flowers again. The female flight attendant pulls the cart past. But, this time a male attendant smiles at Aunt June and myself. He smells like bubblegum and hand sanitizer.

"What can I get you, honey?" he asks Aunt June.

Aunt June orders another Diet Coke. The man hands

her the cold beverage, but he doesn't pull on the tab this time. Aunt June's polished pink, thick, yellowed nails, dig for the metal release tab. *Pop...Fizz.*

The flight attendant pushes the trolley another row down: clinking with mini bottles of vodka, rum, soda cans, hot coffee, and juice. Behind us, across the aisle, I can hear the man in the white cowboy hat speak.

"Just a water please," was all he requested from the male attendant.

I hear a high-pitched, bubbling, wheeze.

My silver fur stands on end, trailing down the back of my neck—a Mohawk stretching the length of my spine. I am panting quicker. Saliva foaming from my open mouth.

Aunt June looks over at me, becoming alarmed. "Buster, what's wrong?"

She digs in her plastic cup, with her painted pink, yellowing fingernails, finding a piece of ice that she offers to me.

Phreeeeeeeet!

My eyes go blurry. I can barely make out the little boy in the striped shirt, scampering down the aisle towards me. Running with the toy airplane between his puckered lips, blowing into the tail end. The front cockpit letting out a high-pitched scream. The toy plane is a whistle.

Phreeeeeeeeeet!

Instinct.

My former training overpowers me. *Disable. Protect. Kill.*

My lips fold under to expose my fangs. Snarling. Bounding over Aunt June, I knock her Diet Coke to the ground. Soda splashes, and pretzels crunch, on the floor under my heavy paws. Taking one more powerful lunge to *disable.* I aim for the small boy's throat. My powerful jaws crushing his tiny neck. *Kill.* My teeth digging deeper into his soft flesh, filling my mouth with hot pumping blood. The boy's neck is hanging limp, only connected by the spinal cord. This feels familiar. I give the broken neck an additional shake for good measure.

"Oh my God, he just blew the whistle!" Betsy bristled, becoming livid with Blake.

He had promised not to blow it on the airplane. His father had purchased the toy whistle when he dropped them off at the Anchorage airport. He was being particularly nice to all of them. Blake had been thrilled with the attention given to him by his daddy.

"Try keeping a three-year-old from blowing a whistle, Jared," she annoyingly reproached him. "I have a two-day trip ahead of me, with two tiny people, and a now a whistle —thanks a lot."

He ignored her as always, hugging and kissing Blake and Clarabelle. Then he leaned into kiss Betsy on the lips, she pulled away, and he laughed at her like it was joke.

———

They made pine tree car scents—claiming to smell like fresh mountain air—that was what Jared smelled like. He would return home from riding the snow machine at breakneck speeds along the crooked spruce tree lined trails. She would bury her face into his chest, sucking in nature's essence like the icing off a cake.

They had met in the Florida Keys five years prior. She was waitressing at The Fat Conch Tiki Bar, after graduating from the Key Largo High School the year before. Jared grew up on the Kenai Peninsula in Alaska but was spending the summer trapping lobster in the Florida Keys with a friend of his fathers.

They were tan, young, and feeling the conch spirit; drinking Captain Morgan's coconut rum and Cokes, lying on the beach under the dancing palm tree shadows, fishing for yellowtail and hogfish, devouring conch fritters and key lime pie, and making love to Jimmy Buffet's rendition of *Brown Eyed Girl*.

―――――――

Here she was on an airplane—the circle of life—returning her to the islands.

Betsy clinched her jaw as she listened for Blake to blow that damn whistle again. Then she felt a sudden *thump* that jarred the plane.

THE CLEAN-CUT FLIGHT ATTENDANT, with the nametag claiming Nicco, handed Buckeye a plastic cup of water with no ice. Buckeye placed the cup of water on his tray, atop the square napkin in front of him, when he heard the screaming of a whistle.

Phreeeeeeet!

He looked up to see a very young male child, wearing a striped shirt, awkwardly running down the aisle, a toy plane whistle squeezed between his lips. The flight attendant followed Buckeye's gaze, turning his body to the front of the plane in order to face the blasting sound. Both men watched in horror, as the massive Pitbull leaped over the elderly frizzy haired woman, landing in the aisle with a crash. It then proceeded to attack the three-year-old.

"Woooo!!!" Nicco screamed, taking several steps towards the ensuing attack.

The dog hearing the flight attendant yelling turned its massive body around to lock its menacing yellow eyes on Nicco. The dog's savage face was dripping with the child's blood, staining the white fur bib on its chest red. Nicco was trapped between the trolley and the snarling dog. Buckeye watched as the dogs protruding muscles started clenching and straining, before it pulled its body back and lunged its mass at the flight attendant. Nicco's body was flung backwards, ramming him against the trolley, pushing the cart down the aisle, just enough to expose Buckeye, now trapped with his tray down, next to the murderous rampage. Buckeye was shocked to see the dog only inches away, ripping and shredding at Nicco's arms. The flight attendant was unsuccessfully fighting off the savage dog.

Get your shit together man, Buckeye ordered himself, cautiously reaching his right hand down to his belt to release the snap closure on his gun holster.

The sound of the snap closure seemed as loud as the kid's whistle but had been drowned out by Nicco's fight for life. The gory scene was playing out on the aisle floor at his feet. It appeared Nicco was losing the battle. One of his arms revealed severed tendons and was hanging by exposed muscle. Blood saturated the blue hall carpet, oozing into his row, forming a puddle under his boots. He eased out his Glock 45, taking comfort with its weighted power.

Nicco stopped fighting, his body slouched against the beverage cart. Buckeye hardly recognized the flight attendant. The dog had made a sinkhole of his face. The man was suffocating on his own blood, making red bubbles around where his lips used to be. Buckeye looked at the blood-soaked animal chewing on Nicco. Its silver fur convulsed with tremors. Screaming and chaos erupted through the plane. Buckeye remained calm listening to the dog's teeth grinding against the flight attendant's bones.

Maybe five rows up, he watched the murdered boy's mother stepping into the aisle. Her dark hair thickly braided to the side wrapped around her neck like a noose. Her worried face contorting into stunned horror, clearly bewildered by the vision of her child's murdered body lying on the aisle floor.

Buckeye focused his attention on the boy's red Converse shoes. Gaining his composure, he glanced back to the grieving woman rooted in the aisle, and noticed she was holding a baby wrapped in pink.

"Did he fall?" she asked the baby.

Turning her head to look back with one eye, peeking through the gap in the seats. She was only able to view the empty seats behind her. Extending her neck to look above the rows, she saw the male flight attendant turning from his cart to face the front of the plane. Betsy watched his face turn ash white with panic. She had already unbuckled her seatbelt when the flight attendant began screaming. Betsy pulled herself up, with Clarabelle sleeping in her arms, quickly maneuvering her way out of the row.

Lifeless on the floor, her precious baby boy's body was splayed in the aisle—his neck drenched in blood. Blake wasn't moving. Behind the boy's motionless body, the massive dog had just taken down the flight attendant. The dog was snarling, generating slurping sounds like he was sucking noodles at an Italian buffet. It ripped at the male flight attendant's face, while holding the trapped man down under its ferocious mass.

She locked eyes with a man wearing a white cowboy hat. He was sitting calmly inches away from the gory rampage. She darted her gaze back to the uncontrollable dog. The dog must have sensed her presence in the aisle way behind him, because it took a break from mauling the man and turned its massive body to face her. Deliberately, it began maneuvering around the flight attendant's corpse. The dog wore a hood of blood. Its yellow empty orbs were floating in a sea of red. Its eyes had fixated on her.

This was the opportunity the cowboy had been waiting for. She watched him awkwardly mount from his cramped seat, stretching himself tall like a praying mantis, aiming a gun at the mad creature. The dog heard the cowboy's knees knock against the tray in front of him, splashing water onto the seats. The mad dog quickly pulled its yellow eyes away from Betsy to look back at the large cowboy, who had positioned himself in the aisle.

It had taken less than sixty seconds for the dog to effortlessly slaughter Blake and the flight attendant. It took the same minute for the elderly, frizzy haired dog's owner, to react to the brutal attacks. The old woman had by now uneasily lifted herself from her seat.

"No Buster. No!" her shaking voice shrieked at the crazed dog.

The dog was standing at attention next to her, with his wrecking ball head turned towards the back of the plane. The dog was concentrating on the gun held in the cowboy's hands; his finger on the trigger. Frantically, the old woman attempted to reach for Buster's collar and restrain him, clumsily her floral muumuu caught on the edge of the armrest, causing her to lose her balance. The woman tripped in the same moment the cowboy fired his gun.

Bang!

The woman—a bouquet of poinsettias—dropped on top

of the maniac mutt, protectively covering the dog's body with her own.

Baby Clarabelle's arms splayed out as a reaction to the sound of the gunshot, but she didn't wake.

Betsy had the urge to run to her broken son. There was a chance he might be alive. Then she watched as the dog began digging its way out from under the woman's flowered body; the dress was now darkening with her blood. The old lady had been shot by the cowboy's bullet.

"Everybody remain in your seats," the cowboy yelled. "Do not move!"

Betsy was quietly crying. Her face wet from the sticky tears and snot. Navigating her way back into row ten, she quietly lowered what remained of her family into the window seat. Keeping her sanity by memorizing every detail of her daughter's angelic sleeping face. Warm tears slid from the corners of her blue eyes and traced lines down her pale cheeks.

She sniffled to Clarabelle, "Don't wake up baby."

BITE YOUR HAND OFF

Her lackluster spirit and waning inspiration had burned out.

Maxine sipped her third mini bottle of white wine from the plastic cup. *Phreeeeeet.*

The sound of a whistle shrieked through the cabin. Maxine's slight hands instinctively rose to her ears.

"Owie. Brunny did that hurt your ears?" She tweeted, sweet talking to the little dog. "Who did that?"

Her dog was now standing uneasily in his kennel. His anxiety prompted his fur to pop out the round breathing holes of the cage. The little guy softly growled. Making his yellow fuzz buzz, reminding her of a bumblebee. She really didn't think much of his ornery disposition; it was on par with his normal bad attitude, she usually sanctioned as adorable.

Phreeeeeet.

Her husband turned his head down the aisle, looking behind them to where the high-pitched sound had come from. She felt a large *thump,* then watched as Max's back turned as rigid as her periwinkle starched shirt. She returned his gaze; his wide-open eyes flashing a warning signal. Undisguised fear distorting the good side of his deformed face.

She felt a large *thump*. When he returned his gaze to look at her, he was as white as a ghost. She would have thought him dead had he not spoke.

"Maxine," he choked.

She couldn't hear him under the drone of the engine.

"What is it Max?" She peeped too loudly.

His finger went to his lips. Shushing her.

"Is it a terrorist?" She questioned him. "A bomb?"

She heard the male flight attendant scream several rows back.

"Woooo!" He let out several long, harsh, screams like a barn owl, "Wooo!"

She heard the airplane passengers begin screaming. The yelling ruffled her nerves. The chorus reminded her of a rabbit's cries as it's carried away in a hawk's talons.

Maxine watched a young mother, her long dark ponytail drawn over her shoulder, maneuvering her body into the aisle. The woman was standing a few seats in front of her, along the opposite side. Maxine could see she was hugging a small infant tightly to her chest, wrapped in a downy rose blanket. The mother's blue eyes became far-reaching, as she tried to spy her toddler son. Maxine watched as the woman's pink cheeks turned sallow, her entire face becoming corpselike. With her flush lips opening wide to encourage a scream, instead, her teeth bit down sharply on the bottom lip, cutting the sob short. A crimson droplet trickled from the gash, running down the side of her chin to blend with the tears. She became the picture-perfect vampire, swaddling a porcelain infant.

Maxine's own heart became a hummingbird—beating 1,200 times per minute against her rib cage.

Bruno let out a high-pitched *Yip!*

Maxine cried out.

The sound of her own shriek was drowned by the screams of the other passengers.

"No Buster. No!" A quivering elderly voice screeched at the dog.

And then they heard the thunderous boom of the gunshot.

Bang!

Her ears were ringing.

Bruno *yipped* and began whining in his kennel. Maxine could see that Max was deeply concerned about the dog making noise.

"What is it, Max?" She asked him desperately under her breath.

Her hands were grasping the armrests. She could see her knuckles turning white. Maxine watched the horrified young mother slink back into her seat without uttering a word. The tears pouring down her cheeks were speaking enough.

"The dog killed the boy and..."

He stopped talking—his eyes becoming louder than his voice—screaming at her to hold her tongue.

"Why isn't anyone doing any..." He stopped her from speaking by reaching out with his hand to cover her mouth.

"Everybody, remain in your seats, do not move!" A man yelled from behind her.

Maxine looked back one row to peer through the space between the seatbacks. She had a front row reclined view of the monstrous scene playing out. The massive bloodied Pitbull was pulling itself out from under its incapacitated elderly owner garbed a red poinsettia muumuu. She saw a man in a white cowboy hat standing next to his seat. He was holding a gun aimed at the dog.

The dog seemingly aware of the gun pointed at it, began crawling into the row on the opposite side, using the limp body of its owner as protection. Maxine could clearly see a middle-aged blond woman, wearing headphones, was sitting next to the window in the row the dog had just entered. The cowboy lost site of the killer dog as it clambered nearer the blond woman. Maxine counted to ten, waiting for the lady to scream, or be killed.

"One, two, three...nine, ten."

Nothing.

"Maybe the dog is injured," she told Max excitedly.

She watched the cowboy stepping over something blocking the way. He had a two-handed grip on the gun, with it extended in front of him in a low-ready position.

"He looks like a cop, Max," she whispered, with her pink lips contorting. "We're going to be okay."

At that moment Carmen, the flight attendant who had been hiding behind the cart, stood up thundering, "Did you kill the dog?"

The cowboy turned his attention back to the beautiful woman asking the question.

The second his focus was displaced, the dog moved on him like a baseball bat striking a homerun. Its mouth was wide-open, one hundred and fifty pounds of twitching muscle advanced on the cowboy. The massive dog's bloodied jaws wrapped around the cowboy's tattooed arm. The sound of cracking bone echoed through the otherwise silent airplane. The bite held enough power to rip off the cowboy's hand holding the Glock; completely severing it at the wrist. Blood began shooting like water from a water gun, drenching the cabin in red.

The cowboy let out a guttural moan, "argh!"

Cradling his arm, he stumbled backwards over what appeared to be more bodies lying in the aisle.

CARMEN WAS CROUCHING behind the trolley. There is no protocol for this.

Holding back tears she silently commanded herself not to scream.

Are there any weapons on the airplane?

No knives, no guns, no mace, no fire extinguishers to hit the dog with, no pocketknives, no Goddamn machetes, no weapons of any sort, and no poisons were on board. She could throw Coke cans at the beast, she mused.

Do I stand up and yell...should I tell everyone to remain calm...do I ask for volunteers to fight off an attack dog...I need to get the first aid kit! All the questions and concerns were jumbled into one thought.

She was looking at the back of the plane. People were starting to stand up to get a better view at what was happening on the other side of the cart. They were looking at her cowering behind it.

"Nicco!" She was talking to herself. "Oh my God, what just happened?"

She made eye contact with a teenage boy, in a yellow

shirt, seated several rows back. He had inflamed red dotted pimples covering his face. He looked terrified.

Then she heard the gunshot.

Bang!

Her ears were ringing.

On the other side of the cart, the man wearing a cowboy hat shouted, "Everybody remain in your seats. Do not move!"

He had a gun. He must be an Air Marshal, she thought.

"Thank God," Carmen traced the cross on her vested chest, keeping eye contact with the pimply boy, she whispered, "We're going to be okay."

She stood up from her crouched position, hiding behind the cart, and was bombarded by the display of carnage in the aisle in front of her. The Air Marshall cowboy was straddling the old woman's poinsettia-flowered corpse with his gun still drawn.

"Did you kill the dog?" She asked the cop, a bit too loud.

He turned to look at her. His rugged mouth shaped the letter O. He looked surprised at the question in the moment. She was registering the bewilderment on the Air Marshal's face when the bloodied dog pounced. He emerged from behind the seats, appearing as large as the giant cop. Its thick muscles flexed as it knocked the cowboy backwards, its jaws powerfully gripping the man's wrist. The cowboy tripped over the old woman, banging his head against the cart, before landing on Nicco's blood-soaked body.

She heard the man cry out.

The hulking blood covered creature had overpowered the large officer. She grimaced, witnessing the dog holding the cop's severed hand in its mouth, still entangled with the gun. Carmen watched the weapon slip from the mutilated cowboy's dead fingers. It landed with a *plop* next to the frizzy haired old woman's head. The dog spit out the chewed up detached hand, before it started to maul the cowboy's shoulder—inching towards his neck. The cowboy, in a fight for his life, started to drag himself into the floor space of the row closest to him, holding his butchered arm close to his body. Scooting. Dragging. All while the dog continued to gnaw at his flesh.

Carmen, in her skirt and heels, sunk back down behind the cart. Her instincts told her to not provoke the dog. She put her finger to her mouth trying to shush the murmurs and the crying she could hear all around her.

Her friend Nicco was dead on the floor, three feet away from her, separated by an aluminum drink cart.

No sudden moves. She knew about aggressive dogs. Rottweiler, Pitbull, and German shepherd guard dogs were commonly found at her friend's and family's homes. She knew dogs could sense fear.

Carmen peeked through the gap between the cart and the seat, looking towards the front of the plane. She could see part of Nicco's shredded arm; a red stream was running down it, flowing into his open blood-filled palm, like a Greek fountain. Nicco's hand pointed to a pair of cowboy boots curled together; the cop had tucked his long body into the row on the other side of the cart. She couldn't tell if he was alive. Looking past her dead friend and past the cowboy boots, she was able to spot the old woman's large flowery body submerged in a blackening pool of blood. The woman's wispy white hair was soaking up the sticky flow, turning it a Cuban favored red-orange hair color.

The boy's body was hidden from her sight by the woman's flowery mound. The dog sat at the side of its deceased owner facing away from her. Its enormous back was caked in gore and what looked like flaps of human skin and tissue. The dog was mourning the loss of its master and guarding the woman's body.

Click.

The sound came from the back of the plane. Carmen's heart skipped a beat as she waited for the dog to respond to the noise. The brute remained next to its owner. Carmen turned to the passengers behind her to see who or what had made the sound. A nice-looking Asian man in designer jeans and a tucked in red flannel shirt had opened the upper storage compartment nearly ten rows back. His daughter looked to be around seven years old. She was dressed in a blue t-shirt, with a picture of a panda on the front.

The little girl was clinging to him fiercely, refusing to let go, as he tried to pry her off. He finally managed to unwrap her fingers from their tight grip. He proceeded to lift her into the air and stuff the her into the storage space above the seat. The girl stopped struggling. Carmen could see snot oozing from her small nose. The man handed his daughter his cell phone to play with and for light, Carmen supposed. Then he reached down to his seat and grabbed a cocktail napkin to wipe her face clean. He *clicked* the compartment shut with his child in it. Lowering himself into his seat, he rested his head in the palms of his hands and shook.

God, please don't let that child suffocate, Carmen crossed herself.

A squeaky high-pitched *yip* screeched through the cabin, sending shivers down Carmen's back. The colossal brute stood and began to pace a few feet up the aisle. Tremors were running up and down its pulsating fur after hearing the tiny Pomeranian dog bark.

God, please don't let that little dog bark again.

The killer dog returned to its spot next to the old lady's body, sitting with his back to Carmen once more.

Carmen turned to face the back of the plane. People were whimpering around her. Otherwise they were being quiet.

She needed to do something now.

DEREK HEARD the commotion coming from the coach section. It started with a piercing whistle...then a *thump*... and a scream.

It could be anything, he thought.

Probably that annoying kid bumped into someone and fell. The little twerp in a striped shirt had come running into the first-class area several hours earlier.

"Get the hell out of here, kid!" Derek promptly scolded him.

He watched the kid take off in his little red shoes, running back to his mom. He hadn't seen the kid again.

The first-class stewardess was a middle age woman with faded auburn hair loosely piled on top of her head. A spare tire had formed around her gut from her age and he suspected a poor diet. She probably consumes excessive amounts of alcohol, he judged by her ruddy complexion, taking a sip from his own gin and tonic.

"They probably gave her the first-class section because she couldn't fit down the coach aisle anymore," he joked to the senator after the flight attendant served him his sixth cocktail. "She should retire."

"Why couldn't we have had that *Carmen* stewardess?" he slurred. "She makes me crack a fat."

Derek was feeling toasty from the mixed drinks. Carmen was the hottest piece of ass he had seen in a while. *Well, since last night at the strip club anyway.*

"Hair of the dog," he held his drink in the air to cheers the senator. "I'm cactus from getting pissed in Vegas last night!"

Then he heard the roar from a gunshot.

Derek had been around long enough to know this was a serious problem. He immediately thought of the 9/11 terror attacks. He had always wondered if all the TSA and Customs security checks were necessary.

"Yeah, apparently they fucked up this time," he trembled.

Derek unhooked his seatbelt and twisted his body around to face the rear of the plane. He was sitting in the last seat in first class and was able to reach his hand over to pull the blue fabric curtain divider an inch to the side to peek through into the economy section.

He saw the kid he had yelled at earlier was dead in the aisle. The red puddle his body rested in matched the kid's red Converse sneakers. A large elderly woman lay incapacitated behind the boy. Behind her, the male flight attendant sat upright on the floor against the cart. The man gazed back at Derek with empty clouded eyes behind a bloody mask. The biggest, nastiest dog he had ever seen was straddling another man who was fighting for his life on the floor of row 15. Derek could see the man's cowboy boots twitching in the aisle as the dog continued to maul him.

Derek's scrutinizing eyes connected with an attractive

young woman, in tall black boots, sitting in the second row of coach. She appeared to be petrified in her seat. He slowly let the curtain slip from his fingers.

"What the hell was that, Beeman?" inquired the confused Senator.

Derek needed to take charge of the developing situation.

The frumpy stewardess, Nancy, came charging out from her galley area to see what the commotion was about. She was walking towards the back of the plane with a chieftain like authority. Derek stood up in the aisle with his legs spread wide and his chest inflated to block her.

"Look we need to barrier off the first-class cabin, NOW," he bored into her hazel eyes, whispering frantically, while pointing to the rear of the plane. "There is a dog attack happening just behind the curtain."

The look on her face showed complete disbelief; she glanced down at his half-empty cocktail sitting on the tray next to his seat. She immediately dismissed his claim. He knew the woman was going to squeeze past him and walk through the curtain to her likely death in the coach cabin.

Derek was a man of action. He reached his arm back, pulling his hand into a tight ball, and punched her in the face as hard as he could. He heard her nose crunch as she dropped back. Derek lunged forward to catch her. At the same time the senator had come out of his seat, and was able help block her tumble by swooping to catch her under the arms, almost falling backwards himself under her dead weight.

"What the fuck?" he sputtered at Derek.

Derek held his finger to his lips, and started frantically making slicing motions across his neck, as he pointed at the curtain separating the coach section.

The senator looked at the curtain and shook his head not understanding.

"Help me get her into the seat man," the senator barked at Derek.

They dragged her into the second row and dropped her into the leather seat.

"A vicious dog is loose on the plane," Derek said under his heavy breathing.

His nostrils flared as he addressed the first-class passengers.

"The dog has already killed several people and it looks like it isn't stopping. It's mauling a huge guy right now. We need to try and block it from gaining access to our cabin."

"That is the most ridiculous idea!" A businesswoman, wearing tortoiseshell glasses, dressed in a blue Armani suit, responded from the front row. "You will just draw more attention to us by making all that noise trying to block the entry. Who made you commander of this ship anyway?"

"Do you have a better idea?" Derek asked her. "If not, I say we start piling up carry-on luggage between the last row seats in first class...slowly and quietly please."

The disgusted businesswoman muttered, "If people need the sanctuary of the first class from being mauled to death, by all means we should allow them in...My God people."

"I don't give a flying fuck what you think," the senator said. "Shut the Hell up."

"This will be on your conscious!" The woman hissed.

"Look lady, if people start to mob towards the front of the plane, the weight distribution will take the damn thing down, and everyone on board," Derek seethed at the businesswoman. "I saw it happen in the Congo."

Derek had been sitting in the open-air airport in

Bandundu, Congo, sifting through a seven-year-old People magazine he had found in the seat next to him. Large groups of people had formed outside the exit of the airport waiting for the plane's arrival. He had been biding his time so he could collect his hired guide. Derek was flying the English-speaker from Kinshasa to help scout out locations for a remake of Joseph Conrad's *Heart of Darkness*.

He watched the plane shift forward as it lined up with the runway. He could tell it wasn't coming in straight. As the pilots attempted to land, the nose of the plane hit the ground before the back wheels, causing the airplane's metal to collapse into burning scraps.

According to the lone survivor, a crocodile had escaped from a passenger's duffel bag during the flight. The reptile caused the flight attendant to run towards the front of the plane, followed by a stampede of passengers, throwing the aircraft off balance. Surprisingly, the crocodile also survived the crash, but was later neutralized by a blow from a police officer's machete. The police never notified Derek to let him know if the guide had perished in the flaming crash; he had just assumed so and carried on with scouting out film locations solo.

Now he had to think of a way to separate the first-class section from coach with more than a thin blue fabric curtain.

He needed a wall.

He tiptoed to the galley frantically looking for something to block the passage. There was no trolley because it was first class and the flight attendant prepared the food and drinks in the galley, but it looked like the food warmers were on wheels and could be wheeled down the aisle like the drink cart. He unlatched the hook holding the warmer in place, pulling it from its designated spot to push it down the aisle. Murphy's Law in place; each rotation of the wheels sounded like the high-pitched squeals of pigs going to slaughter.

Squeak! Squeak! Squeak!

He stopped the cart at the last seat and locked the wheels in place. The senator had started to unload the carry-on luggage from the above storage compartments and began passing hard shell Samsonite bags to Derek, who crammed the pieces between the open gaps along each side of the cart.

ALL DOGS DON'T GO TO HEAVEN

Nick wished he were sitting in the window seat, instead of the aisle seat he requested. The initial attack on the little boy happened just inches behind him. He watched the back of the rock-solid dog's skull mutilating the child, before he squeezed his eyes tightly shut. Nick did nothing to help the boy. The man with the ponytail sitting next to him did nothing either.

Yip...yip...yip! The little freaking dog barked again.

Nick was too afraid to turn around and see the carnage from the ruthless rampage. After hearing the passengers' screams, then the sound of a gunshot, the plane had become eerily quiet. It was like people knew the dog was the predator and the passengers the prey.

Nick closed his eyes; his fingers began stroking the cross pendant, hanging from the gold chain around his neck.

"God help me live through this senseless slaughter."

Soundlessly Nick began rocking his head back and forth, as the Holy Spirit whispered his heavenly dialect through him.

Nick had been strong in his convictions, but recently he

had questioned his faith and his actions. Could he have been wrong about vaccines...did *Green Juice Protocol* really save lives and heal cancer like Drew had told him...did it matter if he purchased organic or non-organic products... was Jesus listening...why did God take his best friend Lola... where does a dog's soul go if it can't enter heaven...could he have prevented her from dying from parvo?

Nick was a staunch anti-vaxxer, even joining demonstrations with other like-minded individuals. He would hold oppositional protest signs at each venue; *Veggies not Vaccine$* and *Vaccinated Kids are Sloughing Diseased Skin onto our Healthy Kids.*

One of his aunts knew a woman whose kid was diagnosed with autism shortly after being vaccinated. He had read the numerous articles supporting his views of big pharmaceutical company's moneymaking schemes. He liked the memes on Facebook. He didn't trust the government, so he didn't trust any of the Centers for Disease Control's lies. He was sure they were trying to poison the population. His co-workers mostly agreed with him, but some friends would make outrageous claims trying to antagonize him.

"Vaccines have saved millions of people's lives from the horrible infectious diseases—polio, measles, typhoid, rubella and smallpox."

"Polio still exists—it's just called a different name!" He posted on Facebook. "Bill Gates is a murderer!"

He opted out of vaccinating his boxer pup, Lola. He felt good about the decision. On his days off from work and church, Nick and Lola would drive to Tahoe for a weekend of biking, Lola pacing him with her exuberant energy. People would comment on how Lola and Nick looked alike, with their fawn colored rich auburn hair, dark eyes, and squashed snouts. They both had athletic builds with muscular frames; funny how dogs could look like their people. Lola had a racehorse metabolism and needed a high protein diet to keep the weight on. Unlike Nick who had to watch every morsel that went into his mouth, eating a high protein diet to keep the weight off.

Lola picked up the crushing parvovirus at the dog park after sniffing poop. The veterinarian rebuked Nick, informing him the disease had been preventable with the vaccine. Lola was hooked to intravenous fluid to help with her severe dehydration, and then a week later she was diagnosed with a bacterial infection, a result of a weakened immune system—and she died.

Nick sought the counsel of his pastor at the Los Angeles Christ First Church, north of L.A. He lived in a suburb apartment complex almost an hour south, but chose to drive to Christ First, because he loved the music and the friendly people. He loved the way they loved him.

The pastor was a recovering drug addict who had found salvation through Jesus Christ his savior. The pastor's entire family would break out in fantastic worship songs, even writing and performing their own biblical lyrics. The youngest son in a suit and tie would play the drums, the next son up in a bow tie played the guitar, and the third son wore a fedora while playing the upright bass. His redheaded wife was on vocals, with their bleach blond tween daughter running the screen projector. The holy songs praising the Lord were displayed for the whole congregation to join in hymn. The spirit would envelope the worshipers; with shy people belting out chorus, business owners speaking in tongues, and old folks holy rolling.

"The only solace I have after Lola's death is that she is with God in a better place," Nick explained the comfort it brought him knowing he would see Lola again to Pastor Rick. "One day I'll be reunited with her in heaven."

The pastor's face turned down in pity and he rested his hand on Nick's shoulder.

"Sorry Nick, but dogs don't go to heaven," Pastor Rick said honestly and forthright while opening his Bible to Revelations.

"In the final chapter of the Bible, it says, 'Blessed are those who wash their robes, that they may have the right to the Tree of Life and that they may enter the city by the gates. *Outside are the dogs* and sorcerers and fornicators and murderers and idolaters, and everyone who loves and practices falsehood.'"

Not seeing Lola in heaven seemed unbearable to Nick. Then with the help of his pastor, he recognized even though he loved his pet fervidly, he could not lead a pet-centered life, his life needed to be Christ centered. He immediately started applying this towards mountain biking, his family, friends, job, alcohol, sex and money—making Christ the center of his life.

He was brought back from his thoughts by the *yipping* yellow dog in the row next to him.

Yip...yip...yip, the Pomeranian let out another high-pitched rapid succession of barking.

He heard and felt the giant dog standing up, taking calculated steps, tramping toward the sound coming from the row next to him. Nick didn't blink an eyelash. The dog was covered in coagulated blood, making his silver fur appear as black as the Angel of Death. The dog sniffed at the air, inhaling Nick's anxiety. It looked at Nick with its flaming amber eyes. Nick turned his eyeballs to look away, out the window at the blue beyond. He could feel the dog's lumbering movements and hear its heavy breathing as it returned to the guard position next to the body of its owner.

Nick took a shallow breath of air and looked over at the man across the aisle with the ponytail and the missing face.

"Shut your dog up Max!" Nick hissed through his teeth.

The man's blond wife bent forward to look at him with loathing.

He watched her lean close to the carrier and begin speaking in hushed tones to the frightened dog, "Brunny please be quiet...baby...sweet Brunny please."

Yip...yip...yip! The dog barked in response to her coddling.

Nick, in blind haste, with zero thought of the consequences, un-lodged his body from his frozen position and reached his torso across the aisle to snatch the dog carrier by the handle. With brute strength Nick flung the cage with the whimpering Pomeranian towards the front of the plane.

"Nooo!" The bird-like woman screamed.

Her hands were desperately grasping at the empty air in disbelief at Nick's unforgivable action. The kennel flew down the aisle landing with a *clump* near the second row of seats. Nick turned his own shocked gaze from the blond bird-like woman to peer up the aisle at the little dog barking wildly in its cage.

Yip...yip...yip!

The cage stood upright between the first and second rows of coach, the right side was occupied by a vixen in black boots, now staring back at him with a look of abhorrence. And on the left side, he held the gaze of a black man, with rage in his eyes. Both passengers were focused on

Nick, not on the little dog barking between them, but on Nick's demonic actions.

"Watch out!" The black man yelled.

The impact felt like being hit by a lightning bolt. He stumbled forward landing chest first on the aisle floor. The bottom half of Nick's body now partially covered the small boy's corpse. The massive dog landed on his back, punching the breath out of him. He felt the canine's razor-sharp teeth ripping into the back of his muscular neck, slicing his flesh with its sharp fangs.

"Help me Jesus!" He screamed out to the silent airplane.

He felt the dog let up and then sink its teeth back into the side of his neck to release his jugular vein. He was drowning in the warm liquid as he sputtered for air.

Nick mouthed the bloody words, "Go to Hell, dog."

With his final thought, he realized he had no idea if dogs went to Hell or not?

THE LITTLE DOG carrier slammed down next to her. The shock almost caused Margot to jump out of her boots with panic. Margot twisted her body to face what was happening behind her and to see who had thrown the small dog. The black father sitting across the aisle had already turned towards the back of the plane.

He then yelled to the ginger meathead, "Watch out!"

She watched as the vicious snarling Pitbull rammed the muscular guy. He crashed onto the aisle floor, landing on top of the dead child. The dog took a deep breath and resumed attacking the man's thick beefy neck for the ultimate kill. When the dog lifted its giant head, its muzzle was covered in blood and flesh. Margot was shocked to see a twinkling gold cross was dangling by a chain from the beast's heaving mouth. #HolyChrist

"Don't go there," she whispered.

The vicious dog in front of her looked just like her family Blue Nose Pitbull, Hugo, minus the gore and the snarling.

The DGT secret memory cursed Margot. She had been sitting on the back patio, soaking up the hot sun, relaxing on the yellow padded lawn chair next to the perfect peanut shaped pool. She nibbled on a #peanutbutterandjelly sandwich with the crusts removed. A glob of the peanut butter, and a dab of jelly landed on her sun kissed inner thigh.

Hugo had been watching her eat the sandwich with an intense desire. He licked his slobbery chops.

She didn't have a napkin.

"Here Hugo...lick it off me," she invited, as she spread her legs to offer him a taste.

Hugo stood at attention, and sauntered over to her, his nut sack squeezed tight between his muscular legs. He licked the sweet, salty goo slowly off her and then began to push greedily for more. His tongue tickled. She giggled. A little more dropped off the sandwich higher up the thigh. He lapped it up with glee; his tail wagged with satisfaction as he pushed himself in towards her. #screwthepooch

What gives you pleasure can thus take it away, she thought about the likelihood of being mauled or killed now that the small barking dog was in such proximity.

Yip...yip...yip, the poufy dog barked wildly, *yip...yip...yip!*

She heard the monster's weight slowly pounding down the aisle towards the tiny dog barking next to her—towards her. Its lumbering black-crusted frame came into her sight. It didn't seem to be in a hurry. It pawed the small dog kennel. Knocking the crate nearly a foot back.

Yip...yip...yip, the little dog barked and started a high-pitched whine.

She knew the big dog was named Buster. Margot had heard the old woman shout the name out before the bullet from the cop's gun had silenced her. Buster let out a rumbling growl. Then began shaking the cage, by grabbing the front metal door with his massive teeth and tossing it back and forth. As the giant dog's head shook the cage, splatters of blood and saliva were flung across the cabin, splattering Margot's arms and face. The little dog was crying out in fear and pain. #BoneBuster

Her heart was thumping so hard she was sure the dog could hear it.

The dog seemingly preoccupied continued to violently thrash the kennel. The cage painfully knocked into her arm causing her to flinch—careful not to cry out—it became too much for her to handle. Margot decided to make a run for the first-class section. Maybe she could reach the bathroom and lock herself in. Maybe that tall, dark, handsome man she saw earlier, sitting in first class, would stop the barbarous animal.

She was panicking. Taking a deep breath, as if she were jumping from a high dive, Margot came springing out of her assigned seat and charged through the blue divider curtains.

#airline#pit#passengers#unsustainable

Ezra was surprised by how calm she felt. Daddy had told her to put her headphones on and listen to the music. She swayed softly while scrolling through her downloaded tunes; she was listening to Bob Marley's *Three Little Birds*.

Marley was telling her not to worry about a thing; his sweet Jamaican beat calmed her nerves. Ezra loved music. Her daddy couldn't afford private music lessons for her, but she joined the band when she entered middle school and was now learning the clarinet. She had been destined to become a band nerd. With her frizzy Afro, thick glasses, perfect academic scores and thrift store clothing she looked like a nerd. Adding the clarinet was kismet. She tapped her gangly legs to the beat, taking time to stare out the window over the green ocean below.

When she turned to look at her father. He was acting strange. She watched him peek down the aisle and then sit back firmly holding the seat's armrests. A drip of sweat slid past his dark eyes, slipping over his round cheek and dropping onto his faded black shirt, leaving a blacker spot. He didn't even wipe off the sweat that still clung to his face.

Her daddy just sat looking frightened, breathing through his open mouth. He felt her staring at him and returned her gaze. She could see the panic by his dilated pupils, in stark contrast to the open white sclera, high-lighting his fear. Daddy smiled at her. It was not a normal smile. It was more of a sneer.

She gasped when a square plastic dog kennel flew above her seat, landing in the aisle with a *thump*.

Yip...yip...yip, the dog in the crate barked frantically. *Yip...yip...yip!*

Her daddy turned to look at the back of the plane again.

"Watch out!" He shouted to someone.

She took her ear buds out and started to ask her father, "What..."

He stopped her with his look. His wide-open eyes were telling her to not speak another word. She held her breath and listened to the little dog *yip*.

Boom...Boom...Boom...Boom, Ezra could feel the steps of someone walking down the aisle.

The little yipping dog's owner she bet.

Then it was like a scene from her worst night terror. The massive dog she was deathly afraid of walked up to the little yellow dog's kennel. The creature was caked in gore. It was growling like a demon from the depths of Hell.

Grrrrrrr.

Warm urine filled the crotch of her shorts and puddled into the seat. The monstrous dog picked up the kennel and started to shake it back and forth. She saw the kennel hit her daddy hard in the shoulder and he bit his lower lip, drawing blood. Then the cage banged against the seat across the aisle. Her daddy didn't move, or make a peep, even while he was covered in splatters of body parts.

The attractive brown-haired woman, who had been

sitting across the aisle, surprised Ezra by darting past the brutal scene. She aimed her slender body for the first-class section but stumbled over the tall high-heeled boots she was wearing, fumbling her attempt to charge ahead.

The woman timed her mad dash, so to slip past the kennel being rapaciously whipped to and fro. Then the lady went headfirst into the curtain that separated the first-class section. Ezra watched the woman rebound off something hard that was blocking the passage. The lady lurched backwards, slithering to the ground in the middle of the corridor, directly in front of daddy, Ezra, and the massive dog.

The demented dog dropped the kennel with its tongue hanging low. It was panting hard from the workout of shaking the Pomeranian like a stuffed toy.

The dog growled.

It braced its paws on top of the crate, using it to as a prop to send off. In the process it wedged the kennel under the front row seat along the opposite side. The demon dog lunged at the dazed woman lying on the ground. The stunned lady locked eyes with the dog, putting her boot out in front of her as it advanced. The long, pointed heel of the boot stuck the animal in the chest. It paused momentarily from the stabbing pain. Then recovering quickly, it reeled back at the woman with increased savagery. She kicked at the beast, but it was already latching its jaws around her booted calf, applying full force and breaking the tibia.

Crack.

Ezra heard the woman's leg bone breaking from the force of the dog's jaws, the leather boot was her only protection from the mauling.

"Ahhhhh," the woman screamed in pain, flailing her body, kicking her legs, in order to free her appendage from the dog's excruciating, bone-crunching grasp.

Ezra watched the lady struggle; finding the moment surreal by her own fascination with the woman's exposed vagina, looking as bare as a baby's butt. She had never seen a woman's privates, and thought it was strange that during a mauling, occurring only feet from her, she would focus her attention on lack of public hair. The pretty young woman was clawing desperately at the first-class wall attempting to penetrate it. The dog let off its grip and the lady kicked at it again with her good leg. The kick nailed the dog directly in the eye with the pointed heel of the boot. Both the woman and the dog looked stunned.

"Arp, Arp," the big dog cried out.

The hurt animal backed off and began rubbing its injured face against the pretty woman's unoccupied seat.

Ezra watched as the lady pulled herself up using the carpeted, plywood wall between coach and first class. She stood with her good leg on the heeled boot, as she dragged the injured one behind her. She continued to push her way past the barricade. The lady persisted by squeezing through an open pocket above the last seat of first class and the divider wall. She began scuffling with someone on the other side. Relentlessly, she pushed back at them. Finally, the lady managed to weasel her body through the hole and into the last row of first class. Ezra heard luggage toppling as the woman disappeared behind the curtain.

THE SENATOR HAD UNLOADED the entirety of luggage from the above first-class storage compartments. He was packing the luggage as quietly as a midnight thief. Stuffing the pieces between the warmer cart and the cracks between the seats. His assistant Stacy had refused to assist him with reinforcing the luggage. She would be promptly fired when this nightmare ended.

He heard a loud *thump* on the other side of the curtain.

"Watch out!" A man yelled a warning to someone.

"Jesus help me!" Another man cried moments after.

Yip...yip...yip, the little dog began barking nearer the curtain.

The senator shivered and started hurriedly piling more pieces of luggage on top of the warmer.

He felt the impact of a body jolting the warmer. He didn't know if it was the dog trying to get past the blockade. He pushed against the warmer from his side, fortifying the already locked wheels. Derek squatted down next to him to help replace the bags that had jarred loose with the jolt.

"Ow," he heard Derek grunt when a hard-shell suitcase

landed on his head, bounced off his shoulder, tumbling behind them.

"That dog is a Goddamn terrorist!"

He heard a young woman on the other side of the curtain cry out in pain, "Ahhhh!"

The rabid dog yelped, and the luggage started to tumble down around them.

"Is it the dog?" The senator questioned Derek excitedly.

"Stop that girl from knocking the wall down," Derek hissed. "She's trying to push through."

"It's a woman, Beeman and I think she's hurt!"

Derek continued to aggressively push her back using a silver suitcase like a war shield.

"She's going to let that dog pass," Derek said, panting.

From his position on the floor, the senator watched as the woman came slithering through a crack in the barrier dividing the first-class section. Derek tried to knock her back, slapping her in the face and body several times with his large hands. But the girl's boot swung over the top of the seats as she came crashing into the last row; the sharp heel slicing Derek across his forehead. He heaved back from the blow, his hands covering his face. When he let off the pressure it revealed a large open gash, blood began weeping down his face into his eyes.

The senator felt nauseous. He had always experienced his emotions through his stomach.

"I need to go to the bathroom." The senator climbed up from his position on the aisle floor where he had been reinforcing the warmer cart and raced to the first-class toilet.

He locked the door. Lifting the toilet seat with sweaty palms, he puked up his numerous cocktails, and some partially digested chicken wings. Afterwards, he sat on the toilet wiping his face with a paper towel. He had never performed well in crisis situations. He did better reading from a teleprompter.

The senator was aware he had been raised a privileged upper-class white kid. His father was a judge. He was provided with expensive private schooling. He enjoyed the upper-class benefits; growing up with summer sailing camps, trips abroad, and an easy acceptance to Florida State University; even with below average SAT scores and a mediocre 3.2 GPA.

His father showed little interest in him, or his poor grades, often responding to his subpar schoolwork with, "You are barely adequate Mike."

Luckily, he was more popular with the kids. He was a handsome light-haired young man who dressed sharply. He played along with the other kids schemes and shenanigans. Always laughing at their jokes.

During Thanksgiving break his freshman year at FSU, he was spending time at his friend Kenny's house, relaxing on the soft leather couches in the den and reuniting with high school buddies. The state-of-the-art screen projector shot the live football game onto the white wall; the players appeared life-size.

Several of the boys started tossing Kenny's family Chihuahua, Bitsy, back and forth to one another. Sometimes using an underhand throw, and then surprising one another with an overhead pass, using Bitsy like a football. The dog cried out, growling and nipping at the boys as it struggled to get away.

"Catch, Mike!" One of the boys tossed her to Mike.

He caught Bitsy around her middle, before turning the

tiny tan dog to face him, its little furry eyebrows raised. Then the pint size mutt lunged with its puny mouth wide open to bite him in the face. Its canine tooth catching on the cheek, as the dog started sliding down it unzipped his flesh, breaking free at his upper lip. He tossed the dog aside and watched it hit the floor, before it went scurrying with its tail between its legs from the den.

At the emergency room the doctor did a butchered job of sewing the sliced cheek and lip together, leaving him with a hair lip gone awry. His father sued the hospital and with the awarded settlement had the jagged line across Mike's face fixed by one of the best plastic surgeons in south Florida.

"What breed of dog was it?" His father had asked him after the mauling. "Was the dog acting aggressively towards you, Mike?"

"The dog was acting aggressively!" Young Mike made it clear to his father. "I swear I didn't do anything to instigate it."

Days later, walking down the marble stairs of his family's five-thousand square-foot holiday home overlooking the white sand beaches leading into the Gulf of Mexico, he heard his father talking into the phone in a hushed belittling tone.

"So, you're saying that an aggressive vicious dog can take my son's face off... have you seen him?" The judge's voice growled. "He is maimed for the rest of his life. It's hard to look at him."

"I will not stop until that dog is put down," the judge jeered the person on the other end of the line. "So, let me get this straight...the other kids are swearing that my son goaded the dog? Are you saying Mike caused this to happen to his face? I'll tell you what...either the dog is euthanized by the end of the week...or you're going to lose everything you own."

The senator sat looking at the *occupied* sign on the locked bathroom door. He was wringing the paper towel in his hands. Maybe he would just sit on the toilet for a while longer and try to settle his nerves and upset tummy.

CLARABELLE STARTED to open her eyes, letting out a "coo."

Her perfect lips forming circles and then relaxing into smiles.

Betsy was concerned the baby would cry, so she opened the side flap of her breastfeeding shirt, pulling out her plump milk-filled teat in a familiar swipe to offer the groggy infant. She was scared to move. All Betsy could do was concentrate on keeping her baby from crying and alerting the dog.

The beast had passed her row again, before returning to guard its owner, several rows behind them. It appeared to have retreated after being hurt by a brown-haired woman, who had made a ballsy attempt for safety, by running for the front of the airplane. It seemed the young woman had fended the dog off with something sharp but had been blocked by a barrier in the divide. She had watched the woman finally worm her way into the safety of the separate section after injuring the gruesome animal.

The bloodied Pitbull's right eye had been gouged nearly out. Betsy could see the upper lid area had turned pink from being sliced open, leaving an empty socket, with a bloody ocular mass of eyeball protruding below.

The dog was a monster.

―――――――

She took comfort thinking about her own good dog. When she adopted him, she thought of all her favorite things and decided to name the pup Salty; like the salty air and the salty ocean, the salty food, and the fucking salty language she loved.

After moving to Alaska from the Keys everyone would ask her, "Did you name him after the Salty Dog Saloon on the Homer Spit?"

She hadn't named him after either an old drunken sailor nor a lighthouse bar covered in dollar bills and women's undergarments.

"It was a funny coincidence," she told them.

She smiled at the memory of moving to Alaska with her dog having the same name as the iconic northern saloon.

One day she heard a song playing on her local NPR radio bluegrass hour.

It was an old recording with a woman belting out a hearty twang: "Let me be your salty dog, or I won't be your gal at all."

What the heck? She thought.

After researching "salty dog," she found that in the olden days people barely had enough money to afford salt for preserving meats, let alone salt for their dogs. When dogs were infested with fleas, people could only spare enough salt for their *favorite* dog. Rubbing its fur with the white granules to help rid the animal of the pesky insect.

Salty dog meant favorite dog. And as sure as shit, he had been her favorite dog.

Some time had passed before the baby started to pull away from her breast. Milk was shooting out at all angles from her swollen nipple. Clarabelle should have been hungrier after sleeping for hours. Betsy wondered if the baby had sensed her own anxiety.

Betsy knew Blake was dead. There was no point in thinking she could save him. She couldn't place these emotions she felt. The grief had been overtaken by survival instinct. She had her entire life to grieve for her small boy. Pulling her right arm out from under the baby, she glanced at her watch; thirty more minutes before they landed. She had thirty more minutes to keep her baby alive.

Betsy could hear the little dog whining and crying in its tipped over kennel that had become lodged under a seat a few rows in front of her. Besides the sounds coming from the small crying dog, the airplane was silent under the drone of the engine.

"Ladies and gentlemen, I have just been informed by our flight attendant, Carmen, the coach cabin is currently under duress. It appears the unfortunate situation does involve a dog. I have been made aware the incident is still underway and not yet contained," the captain's voice blared over the intercom.

"Please do not panic...the seatbelt sign is on...stay in your seats. We are currently flying over the Gulf of Mexico. It will be nearly twenty-eight-minutes before we land in Miami. Ground crews, the proper authorities, and ambulances have been notified of the emergency. They have been dispatched and will be waiting for us upon landing."

The dog started to bay. His low howling drowned out the captain's voice.

"Arh-wooooooooooo," the beast bellowed. "Arh-wooooooooooo."

Betsy could hear the people's nervous movement and the shushing throughout the cabin. The dog had spooked the passengers. It had spooked the baby. She watched Clarabelle's arms splay out—a frightened reaction to the loud howling sound.

Then the baby took her deepest breath, scrunching her face into a bright pink chubby ball, and released a gut-clenching wail.

SICK AS A DOG

MAX FROZE when the red headed son-of-a-bitch, Nick, reached across the aisle and grabbed Bruno's kennel, tossing it with his macho strength out of sight and out of reach.

He had heard the kennel bang, landing hard near the front of the plane.

"Don't move, Max," Maxine voice made a high-pitched nasally sound from the snot filling her nose.

No need to worry yourself, Max thought.

Max hadn't moved a muscle when the big dog gruesomely attacked Bruno's redheaded assaulter from the seat next to him. He became mesmerized by Nick's shirt changed colors like a mood ring, from its original bright red to opaque blood black. Max's feet sat motionless in a deep puddle of Nick's juices. Max hadn't moved a muscle when the savage dog shook little Bruno's cage. Even as his own little dog whimpered in pain. Max didn't twitch a fiber of his being, as the attractive young woman fought off the repulsive dog, before disappearing behind the safety of the curtain.

Maxine was crying next to him.

"Don't move Max," she breathed through her mouth. "Why is this happening? Is Bruno okay? Can you see him?"

"Shhhhhhh," he held up his pointer finger to quiet her.

He peered down the aisle behind them. Max was strapped to his seat, sitting in the heart center of a wolf's den. His redheaded neighbor's brawny body covered part of the dead child; both lay on the floor next to Max. The mad dog was panting through its pain from the eye injury. He sat in the aisle, only two seats behind them, guarding his person.

"If no one moves, and no one makes a sound, we can make it through this," he whispered to Maxine. "There is only half an hour of flight time remaining."

Yip...yip...yip! Bruno chirped out. *Yip...yip...yip!*

"Thank God he's alive!" Maxine exhaled the breath she had been holding.

Max would often find himself weighing out his many options for dying. What would be a worse way to die than by cancer? Would it be easier to have no legs with the chance of a future? Would he rather be blind? Or die in a car accident quickly... or an elephant stampede...by snakebite...slowly with no water in the desert...fast and unexpectedly jumping out of a plane with no chute? What is worse...living with depression and not living...losing a child or a lover to suicide...by carbon monoxide in a vehicle watching the final sunset...a bullet to the head?

"Anything seems better than knowing you will die in a couple of years," Maxine had cried. "Nobody should know their own future."

"We do know our future...we all die, *little bird*. How I

look at it, is at least we have a few years to prepare and check off items on our bucket list." He had comforted her by brushing back her baby soft hair with his big dry hand.

Their newly purchased home was waiting for them in the Castle Valley community, nestled in an ancient red sand bowl, with the Colorado River weaving its way past the green valley, down the enormous red walled canyon, leading to the Grand Canyon below. Freshwater flowed from the La Sal mountain range. The underground aquifers were not yet empty. The long warm months would allow the growing season to be extended as long as ten months.

The replacement home was a sienna colored adobe house surrounded by a mixture of apricot and peach trees from an earlier orchard that had been subdivided. The property came with irrigation rights; every other day a gushing stream of water would flow through a small manmade creek weaving through their yard. They had planned to return to Utah with their belongings after the house closing.

He had so much to do before he died. He still needed to get the water filter systems put in place on the desert property. This way they could always collect rainwater in the barrels that were connected to the house gutters, or if worse came to worse they could collect water from the Colorado River. He was going to start keeping bees. Utah was the Bee State; honey would be great for trade and general survival. He needed to build a chicken coop. He needed seeds for the garden. He wanted to start building a cellar to keep potatoes and other root vegetables, along with canned and jarred items. He could also keep his preppers' stash of MREs and fifty-pound bags of beans and rice in the cellar.

He needed to purchase a large safe to keep all his guns and ammo locked. He had already acquired massive amounts of ammo at a Florida gun auction for future trade and possible defense. He planned to invest in bottles of whiskey, because they lasted for a long period of time...and were great for trade.

With the missing jawbone, he had lost a substantial amount of weight and muscle mass. He was weak and appeared hunched over. Max had always been a strong provider, endlessly moving, and always working. Maxine didn't look at him the same anymore.

"Now, it's like when we were raising Robby," she had said while making Max his pureed dinner. "Of course, the blender is much better than that old-fashioned food mill I used to make his baby food with."

Now when Max would eat, he would asphyxiate, gasping for air, as he choked on the soft food. After each bite he would clean the mess from his face with a handkerchief. Digging into his manmade mouth, with his big fingers, to locate any food that might have been stuck in the hairy cheek pockets. He would never take Maxine out for dinner again. He could no longer perform pleasure on her with his mostly missing tongue. It would be impossible to kiss her passionately ever again. Now, when he spoke sweet nothings into her ear, the whispers reverberated like the babble of a drunken sailor.

Yip...yip...yip! Bruno kept barking from up the aisle.

He heard the loudspeaker vibrate the cabin. It was the shrill sound of the captain's calm and collected voice speaking from behind his secure cockpit door.

"Ladies and gentlemen, I have just been informed by

the flight attendant the coach cabin is currently under duress."

His report felt like an understatement. The captain's voice dominated the cabin, which caused the big dog to become more agitated. It was probably from the screeching volume from the speaker that had interrupted the dead air silence, subsequent to the initial killings.

"Please do not panic...the seatbelt sign is on...stay in your seats," he heard the captain's voice calmly command. The massive hulk started to pace next to his seat, stepping on the bodies as it passed.

The dog was panting, with its tongue hanging from the side of its mouth. Its eyeball dangled by an optic nerve, like a swinging tetherball, while it guarded the aisle. The dog stopped to perch its front red stained paws on top of Nick's red-shirted broad back that lay dead on the floor next to Max. Nick's neck appeared to be nearly severed. The dog had ripped the muscle, bone, and skin from his neck revealing his spinal cord. Blood was splattered through the cabin when it ripped at the man. Chicken pox red spots dotted Max's face and arms.

The dog released a tiger's roar in response to the loud-speaker.

"Arh-woooooooo," it bellowed and then again, "Arh-woooooooo."

Max heard the baby let out and heart-thumping wail.

"Waah," she yowled. "Waah!"

The big dog released a low rumbling growl. Its hackle went on end—each hair tingling and erect. It crept slowly off the man's dead body. Advancing towards the baby's angry cries, coming from only a few seats in front of Max.

"Waah!"

Max thought about leaving his *little bird,* Maxine—all alone in the bullseye of a hurricane—no one to save her.

"I love you, Maxine," he reached out to grab her slender hand tightly in his own.

He looked into her pale blue eyes, wrapped in a murder of dainty crow's feet, decorating her soft skin. Her smooth laugh lines, narrating her pink silky lips, that he used to kiss with total abandonment.

He wondered if this was going to hurt. He wondered if this would be a better way to die; better than the emasculating, drawn out cancer route, that before this flight was his predetermined fate. He didn't want to succumb to the dog, but this day was as good as any.

Pulling his hands from her grasp, he reached out and took hold of the knitting needles she had placed in the middle seat pocket. Holding one needle in each hand, he heaved his frail body into the aisle. Taking one large step over both the redheaded man and the small boy. His foot clumsily crashed onto the aisle floor directly behind the dog. The animal had already stopped next to row 10. It had been staring menacingly at the woman and her small infant. The loud bang made the beast cock its head to assess the sound behind it, directing its full attention on Max.

Max looked into row 10 and locked eyes with the quivering young mother. Her hand was covering the baby's mouth—smothering the infant—to keep her from crying out.

"Hey, Dog!" Max yelled, tempting his own destiny.

It needed to turn its body from its position aimed at the terrified mother and child in order to attack Max. Max decided to take the opportune moment to take the offensive. Striking the dog from behind, he jabbed the knitting needles into each of its tender sides, like an ice climber picking his route. However, the dull needles didn't puncture the skin.

Instead, the enraged dog cried out from the prodding thrust.

"Aarp." In one acrobatic motion, the irate dog flipped its body, a full rotation from its standing position. It landed like a hammer, immediately aiming for Max's jugular. Max shoved one of the needles out towards the dog in an attempt to slow it down, taking aim at its one good eye with the other needle. The first needle pushed into the dog's stomach, causing the animal to lurch forward from the pointed pressure to its gut. The pain precipitated the dog dropping to the ground, causing Max to miss with the second needle that he had aimed at the dog's good eye.

He heard the baby scream out in anger, accusing her mother of fowl harm.

"Waah...Waah!"

The dog took a moment to observe Max and the needles he still gripped in his large hands. It attacked Max again. Max dropped the needle. He balled up his fist and punched at the dog's massive box head. Making contact with the dog's face felt like punching a brick wall. It didn't even flinch. It grabbed Max's ankle and pulled his feet out from under him. He landed on the redheaded man and the small child. Buster landed on Max and proceeded to rip his throat out.

"Maxie!!!" He heard his *little bird* caw.

THE CAPTAIN's announcement might have been a mistake. Prior to the loudspeaker interruption, the passengers had a moment of peace, with the dog taking a break next to its deceased owner.

Carmen decided to take advantage of the resting dog. She checked to make sure the cart's wheels were locked in place in case the dog shoved against it, and to support Nicco's body. Carmen was not naive; the *pit* breed could easily jump over the cart at any time, if it so desired. Her friend Annette kept her Pitbull on a cable runner in the backyard. A six-foot fence surrounded it that the dog could easily jump over had it not been tethered to the cord. The dog could actually climb walls.

Carmen slipped off her high-heeled shoes and quietly began crawling on her hands and knees towards the back of the aircraft. As she progressed down the aisle, she made eye contact with the terrified passengers on each side of the aisle. She tried to soothe their concerns by acknowledging their distress, before she realized her own creased brows were registering the same alarm as the passengers. She could hardly console people while crawling on the ground, cowering beneath them.

An old man, his skin the texture of an elephant, wearing a neck pillow covered in brightly colored fishing lures, leaned his head into the aisle to asked with a shaky voice, from age or trepidation, "Can I help you, ma'am?"

"Please stay in your seat sir...it's safer," she whispered to him. "I'll let you know if I need help."

Carmen assumed Nancy, the first-class flight attendant, would have called in the emergency situation to the captain by now, but all the same she needed to make contact with the cockpit. Once she made it past the lavatories at the back of the plane, Carmen pulled herself around the corner of the kitchen galley. She stood on her bare feet and clutched the phone from the wall receptacle, before dialing the cockpit.

"Captain! Has Nancy alerted you to what is happening?" She asked as soon as he answered.

"I'm sorry Carmen?" Captain Morgan raised his voice. "What are you talking about?"

"Captain we have an out of control dog rampantly killing people in the coach section!" She hissed into the phone. "I know at least five people have been attacked so far —I can't check on them—it's too dangerous. Nobody can move from their seats or they're immediately attacked."

"Is anyone hurt or needing medical attention?" The captain densely asked her.

"Captain...nobody can move or they are attacked!" She cried, squeezing the phone until her knuckles lost blood circulation. "Have you talked with Nancy?"

"No Carmen...she hasn't called. Didn't you say the dog wasn't killing people in first class?"

"Yes sir, only in the front of the coach section so far...

what should I do to help the passengers?" She said drawing her breath. "Nicco...and a little boy...and an old lady...and a cop are all dead sir...how much longer until we land?"

"Oh God, Carmen. I need you to remain calm for the passengers. I'm going to make an announcement to have people stay in their seats. You stay where you are and make sure nobody moves. I'm going to get us to Miami as fast as I can."

The captain clicked off.

Carmen looked around the galley for anything she could use to fend off the deranged creature. She opened a drawer containing trash bags. She could try and smother the dog with a bag. She envisioned sneaking up behind the creature and pulling the plastic bag over its head. Her imagination then played out the scene with the dog's teeth slashing through the thin plastic and so on. She looked up at the overhead compartment above the last row in coach. Row 33; with the three empty seats held in the upright position, permanently pressed against the bathroom wall. The overhead storage compartment held the emergency first aid equipment. Maybe it held something that could be used for defense. Should she chance making noticeable movement in the cabin, in order to get a bag that *might* have something for her to use as protection?

Then, it occurred to her; maybe she could use the defibrillator as a weapon.

She quietly tiptoed, sliding her body along the bathroom door; the sign read *vacant*. She lifted her arm to quietly unlatch the handle lock on the upper cabinet.

Click, it sounded loud like a gunshot, even blanketed by the hum of the airplane's engine.

She paused and waited for any shift from the dog. Then she let the compartment door slide open. Extending her slight body to lift the large bag out of the high space, she spotted the smaller yellow bag next to it. Grabbing the smaller yellow demo bag instead, she hugged it to her chest. Leaving the compartment door open, not wanting to take the chance to alert the dog by making a second *click*. She slowly backed up against the bathroom wall, side-stepping her way into the relative safety of the galley. Carmen placed the yellow bag on the floor and unzipped it. It contained the demonstration items for the safety announcement at the beginning of the flight.

"Nothing in the safety briefing on how to respond to an attack dog," she muttered. The lack of preparation the airline had given her for something like this angered her.

She pulled out the life preserver.

"What can I do with this?" Holding the preserver, she answered her own question, "Maybe hang myself."

Then she heard the beast start to howl.

"Arh-wooooo."

It moaned a sorrowful tune. It sounded like a cry for his lost friend.

She pulled duct tape from the bag.

He was a trapped dog. That meant he was probably a scared dog.

"Arh-wooooo."

Then the baby started to cry. She could hear the baby's wails all the way in the back of the plane.

She reached into the bag and pulled out the weapon of choice—the only choice. The dog was probably going to kill her.

She heard a commotion at the front of the coach section and then the heart-fluttering scream.

"Maxie!!!"

She reached for the phone and attempted to ring Nancy in first class.

Brnng, brnng, brnng...

A husky female voice answered the ring on the other end; she didn't sound like Nancy.

"Nancy is that you?"

DARNELL HAD BEEN FORMING a plan to save his daughter from the massive demon *pit* when he heard the baby start to cry. Ezra was his world, and he was going to save her, but the thought of another child being killed made him rethink his initial plan. This dog was a hell of a lot more bite than it was bark.

On a hot July night, thirteen years prior, he had brought home the newborn Ezra. Home to their bi-monthly, seedy Vegas hotel room, in a desperate part of town.

He made the nappy-haired infant a soft bed in the bottom of the hotel dresser drawer. The baby's mattress was a pillow from the bed. Rolled up towels were installed around the plywood board edges to form a padded bumper. He wrapped her tight in the yellow blanket donated by the hospital; along with two cases of infant formula, bottles and diapers.

"I named you Ezra after your Mimi," he told her. "She

was the first one to graduate high school in the family. I knew you was gonna to be as smart as her."

Darnell's original plan had been to grab the little dog kennel, and distract the demon *pit,* by tossing the crate to the back of the plane. While the demon was busy with the diversion, he would assist Ezra through the barrier into the first-class section. From his front row economy seat, Darnell had watched the first-class passengers jury-rig a blockade, using carry-on luggage and a food warmer. He reckoned it would be easier if he pushed her through the left sidewall of suitcases and over the back seat. She would then drop safely into the final row of first class—the same route as the booted young woman took.

"Waah!" The baby cried. "Waah!"

He loved to tell his daughter stories from the past.

"You screamed for your mama that first night," he would tell her. "I pulled you out of that draw and I held your sweet little open mouth to my bare-chested nipple. You latched on for a second...and then let out an almighty scream...we both know there was no foolin' you!" He would laugh from deep in his belly. "After that we figured things out."

Darnell hadn't been able to get his young bride, Ezra's mother, Glenda, to breastfeed the starving infant. Even after the nurses had explained how important the first few days were for bonding and passing the mother's immunities to the baby.

Ezra's mother had become despondent from post-partum depression. She lay facing away from Darnell and the infant child, staring deep into the faded gold, flowered hotel wallpaper. Sometimes her eyes would flutter, as she peacefully slept the days, the months, and years away. Not much had changed in the past thirteen years.

Darnell thought about earlier that morning when he said goodbye to his wife, while Ezra and he were leaving for the airport. Glenda had been as aloof that morning as the day they had brought Ezra home more than a decade earlier.

"Ezra and I are taking off to Miami, Glenda," he said, leaning on the doorframe of their dark bedroom. "Call me if you need anything. We'll be back in one week...next Tuesday."

She had remained silent.

"Bye, mom," Ezra said when she walked past the bedroom with her suitcase in tow, not slowing a beat. Ezra seemed almost as distant towards her mother these days—as far as the moon and back—as her mother was all the days of Ezra's short life.

Darnell glanced back after hearing a man's garbled voice yelling to the demon *pit*. In the time it took for him to turn his body and face the rampage, the massive dog was already tugging the throat from the ponytailed man with the missing face.

"Maxie!" He heard the man's wife screeching.

Darnell knew this was his moment to act. The crying baby and his girl Ezra were going to get killed if he didn't move fast. He heard the baby cry out again. He decided to reach across the aisle to snatch the small crate jammed under the seat.

As he stretched his beefy arm the two-foot distance, peering over his shoulder at the dog. The butcher animal was approaching the crying baby, all the while glaring directly at Darnell, with yellow menacing eyes.

Darnell began yanking on the dog kennel, but it was lodged tightly under the seat. He reached over with his other hand and started pulling with both of his arms. His excessive gut cutting into the armrest as he struggled to free the wedged dog kennel.

"Arumph," he pulled back and the kennel came free, with the little dog *yapping* at Darnell. Clearly, the puffy dog was sensing this was a sinister move by the large man, and recognized it was not that of kind helpful stranger.

Yip...yip...yip!

Darnell propped the cage in front of his feet, reaching his stumpy fingers around the release lever of the metal grate kennel door. It popped open with a *clink*.

"Get out dog!" He commanded the animal and shook the cage a few times.

The dog would not budge. It backed further into the kennel, trying to escape the giant man roaring at it. Darnell looked back again to see the demon creature had progressed forward; it was now standing menacingly only three rows behind him, next to the row with the crying baby.

"Daddy!" Ezra cried out, reaching to grab his arm with her long thin fingers. "Don't hurt the little dog."

He was already reaching his meaty hand into the kennel, pulling the yellow dog out by its scruff in one aggressive swipe. The little dog growled and *yipped*, biting him on the pointer finger and drawing blood.

"We need a distraction from us, and that little crying

baby, Ezra," he calmed her with his rationality. "One for all."

He stood and tossed the squirming little mutt like a football over the offensive lineman dog's head, aiming for the pile up of dead bodies.

"The little yapper should keep that demon *pit* busy for a while."

STACY HAD GROWN up around aggressive dog breeds. She knew them well. She understood Pitbulls were designed to be guard dogs and or fighting dogs. Her uncle had to pay additional insurance on his house because he owned two Rottweilers. The dogs were a liability, even if they were the nicest dogs in the world. The service dog in coach was doing exactly what the Pitbull was bred by humans to do. She snorted.

Stacy wasn't worried about herself being killed by the animal, sitting in a window in the safety of first class. She had heard the economy passenger's cries coming from behind the curtain. The tormented screams blending with a small dog's continual barking.

"I thought airlines were all about safety," she groaned sarcastically, under her breath to the businesswoman across the aisle. "They got rid of peanuts, because they were dangerous...but Pitbulls are fine to fly!"

She assumed there were enough "bait-dogs" behind the curtain to keep the beast busy, like the ones she kept hearing barking and crying.

Stacy had watched the senator run to the bathroom feigning sickness.

Good move, she thought.

Behind her she could hear world traveler, Mr. Derek Beeman, tending to the injured booted woman. The girl had balls for breaking down the wall, and entering their safety zone, with that dog on her tail.

"Here, Margot. Let me help you rest your leg on this blanket for padding," Derek told the pretty young woman. "We should keep it propped up."

He was probably feeling bad for belting her across the face as she ran terrified for her life, seeking refuge in first class.

"Thanks Derek. Mmm. That feels so much better." The girl swooned in pain. "You will protect me, won't you? I'm so scared."

"Absolutely. Here let me help you up here. How does that feel?"

"Oh!" she heard the booted newcomer gasp quietly.

The young woman sounded startled—caught off guard —by something Derek had done.

Stacy was quitting her job the second the senator returned.

She glanced over at the unconscious, bruised, and abused flight attendant. She could see a darkening mark forming on the woman's cheek.

"Not much I can do for her," she muttered.

She was feeling a little guilty for just sitting in her seat while people were being killed behind the curtain.

Brnng, brnng, brnng.

Stacy heard the buzzing coming from the kitchen area. She unbuckled her seatbelt and removed her heels. Standing quietly, she tiptoed barefoot into the galley area.

The wall phone buzzed, with the bulb blinking red, the phone continued to ring unobtrusively.

"Hello?" She whispered.

"Nancy is that you?" The woman on the other end asked.

"No, this is Stacy, I believe Nancy is currently resting in a seat."

"Excuse me? What did you say?" The flight attendant demanded. "I am going to need her help!"

"She isn't available right now. Is there something I can help you with?" Stacy asked the concerned flight attendant.

"We can't let any more people die! I'm going to do something crazy and I need you to help me. I'm apparently the only flight attendant left...I'm Carmen."

Sounding wary of her own plan, Carmen asked, "Do you know how to whistle?"

Stacy did know how to whistle.

It was predestined, she supposed, that the most devastating moment of her life should be triggered by the request for a whistle, in the midst of a canine catastrophe.

Stacy and her ex-husband had decided to take a holiday. Departing from their usual sailing excursions, they instead chose to drive their Volvo on a month-long cross-country road trip. Ten days into the holiday, they stopped among the red rock canyons of the southwest.

Stacy, her ex-husband, and their dog Chance set off on a sunset stroll along one steep canyon ledge. Walking the top of ancient rocks that jutted hundreds of feet into the heavens, forming islands in the sky, towering over deep dark canyons. They let the dog run ahead, chasing squirrels, and sniffing rabbit holes. It had been a long road trip, driving several thousand miles from Tallahassee to hit up all the most famous sites along the way. They had gone out of their way to enjoy photo opportunities at the largest rubber band ball and the world's biggest corn maze.

Chance needed to release the pent-up dog energy from the long ride. He had been gone for a while. The trees had begun turning to black shadow creatures. The earth darkening under the quickly emerging twilight, with the vivid red rock outline in the far distance a reminder of the days end. The glowing half ring of a crescent moon joined the far-off North Star to welcome the night.

They had circled back along the bluff. A large canyon expanse stretched between where they stood and where they had come from. It looked like a black ocean between two islands. Fixating her gaze across the dark ocean canyon, she waited to see any movement from her furry white and brown mutt.

"Chance!" Her ex yelled out to the dog. "Here boy!"

Stacy raised two fingers to her mouth and whistled, *Whewwwwww!*

On the far-off ridge they could just make out the white of his fur bounding towards them. The bright red sliver of the last of the sun's rays sliced the skyline behind him. Chance was running straight for them.

With her voicer raising an octave, she asked, "Does he see the canyon between us?"

"Excuse me? Stacy! Are you able to help distract the dog?" Carmen brought her back from the disturbing memory of watching Chase fall the near five hundred feet to the bottom of the dark abyss.

"Yes Carmen...I can whistle," Stacy decided to assist the flight attendant.

Apparently, the animal was triggered by the high-pitched sound.

Then Stacy heard a commotion coming from the first-class cabin. She leaned her body out from the galley to see what was happening.

Derek and the pretty young first-class immigrant, Margot, were both fighting off a young African American girl, who was attempting to squirm her way through the opening above the seat. Derek was body-checking her back into the coach section, using the gunmetal suitcase as a shield. The young booted woman was beating the younger girl over the top of her head with a rolled-up Freedom Airlines Magazine.

Stacy was relieved to avoid becoming part of the mounting situation. Returning to the phone, she held it to her ear, "I can skip the whistle Carmen...we have a distraction...and you better hurry."

THE MUTT'S NUTS

It almost felt like I was playing. Shaking the mini wolf-descendant Pomeranian, trapped in its kennel. I just wanted to shut the dog up. It was like a game...breaking into the cage...and then the prize was breaking its neck. I wanted to floss my teeth with the scaredy cat's toothpick bones. I was defeated in my attempts to end the high-pitch *yip*, and the poufy dog continued barking from the safety of its plastic cage.

The suffocating smell of ammonia from a human's urine clobbered my nose, overwhelming the piss and shit released from the *mini wolf* during my aggressive harassment.

The booted woman shouldn't have run from her seat. I would have killed her if she had not hurt me so badly with the claw heel. I could still taste the shoe leather lingering on my pallet. I rubbed my dangling eye against the seat cushion. *Ow*.

I could not tell who on the airplane threatened my Aunt June. Anyone who moved I considered my enemy...and I would make them my prey. I am Buster, the descendent of my wolf forefathers. Human-engineered to be more brutal, to be more loyal, more intelligent, and more vicious.

What would Cindy want me to do? I wondered. I was befuddled by the split in my former training as a protector dog, having just been recalled by the sound of a whistle, and my more recent training to be a Service Dog. I was feeling an internal conflict; the urge to answer a human designed call...from the wild.

After the woman hurt me, I returned to guard Aunt June. I listened for the comforting beat of my companion's heartbeat. Nothing. She had been murdered. I felt unbearably alone. Trapped behind enemy walls. I wouldn't fail her again. The airplane continued buzzing in my head like an annoying gnat. The stifling smell of plastic was making my mind spin. The baby started to wail. I needed to end it.

Approaching the crying infant, I took measured steps over the bodies prone throughout the aisleway. I was focused on ending the grating cries.

Stopping in my tracks, I became riveted by the toothpick dog flying over my head—no longer constrained to its kennel. It landed on its owner's dead body, before jumping up to freely run around my Aunt June. I immediately turned my attention to disabling the *mini wolf*.

I became distracted by a sudden commotion at the front of the plane that instantly rerouted my aim. I must proceed with the mission: disable any threat, protect Aunt June, and kill anything in my way to do so.

My head was throbbing.

My attention turned on the heavyset black man. He had just moved from his seat. I immediately chased him down like a dog. He didn't see me coming. His body was turned away. Siccing the man, I tore into his back. My wet mouth tinged with the warm metal flavor, while I gnawed on his shoulder. I missed his neck from my distorted vision; the injured eyeball knocking against my cheek. The good eye was hindered by an angry throb beating my skull. Not from the man's fists trying to bat me off—human fists don't faze me—but from an ache caused by the high frequency airplane racket.

The man turned his body to face me, ripping away his shoulder flesh from my fangs. He reached down with his meaty paws to grab my front leg. My jaw locked around his thick lower arm. I started to shake it. But he was strong, and held as tightly to my leg, before giving it a brutal twist. We both heard the sound of the bone popping. My jaw automatically released from the unbreakable bite I had on his arm.

Grrrrrr.

The pain caused my remaining one eye to gush tears. I re-stabilized myself with my three spare legs. I was shaking my head to-and-fro, so I could see more clearly.

Whewwwwww!

A whistle.

They say dogs don't see red—that was all I could see.

There was something inside of me feeding the savagery. I was doing what I had been trained for. It was my animal instinct. Accomplished through rigging the wolf DNA—ferocity is what I had been made for.

I reached down to steal one more mouthful of fatty muscle from the man's chest. Chomping on it, my radar scanned for the sound maker.

The man I chewed on continued to moan. A mouth full of his meat dropped from my panting chops, saliva blending with blood to form long pink mucus tentacles, swinging from my open jaws.

The sound came from above the seats, near the trolley at the middle of the plane—near my Aunt June.

Whewwwwww!

My eye blurred. I burst down the aisle, temporarily forgetting I had been maimed. I tripped over the pile of dead bodies; sliding down the corpse mound. I was sputtering and flinging blood about the cabin. Quickly hopping back up to aim my imposing frame at the blinding sound. Snapping my razor-sharp teeth. I leaped for the woman, Carmen—I knew who it was by her smell—jasmine flowers.

I loved Aunt June. I would give my life to protect her. I am a GOOD dog.

It had been her daddy's idea to attempt an escape to the first-class section. She had wanted to stay in her seat like the captain had requested.

"Ezra get up and squeeze your body through that hole right there," he had whispered to her, pointing his big gashed finger to the left of the curtain. "I'm gonna help you...don't worry."

The dog had attacked her daddy, as they battled the walled off passengers, trying to access their impenetrable high-class fortress. Ezra stopped struggling when she no longer felt his protective embrace—he had released her and fallen away. She turned around to find him being mauled by the ferocious dog. Ezra was paralyzed with fear, unable to move from her anchored position standing in the blocked corridor. Her daddy rolled about, writhing at her feet, fighting the beast off with all his might.

Then the beast was called by a whistle.

She slid to the floor and sat with her legs crossed next to her daddy. He moaned in agony from the crater size bite wounds covering his back and arms.

"Lord knows why anyone would purposely call that dog," Ezra said to her daddy, her voice quivering.

With her long, thin trembling fingers she inspected her own face. It was puffy and tender to the touch from being repeatedly smacked by those people in first class.

She and her daddy became shaking leaves on a Weeping Willow during a hurricane.

"That lady will save us." Ezra marveled at Carmen's heroism.

She was dabbing at her daddy's forehead with a paper drink napkin.

He moaned loudly.

"I'm so sorry Ezra," he cried. "I shouldn't've done that."

She calmed him with her long soft fingers by gently caressing his face.

"I love you daddy...we'll be okay."

The second whistle had caused the dog to heave its barrelhead high in an attempt to track the loud sound. Taking a chunk from her daddy, the beast released him from its trenchant bite. The dog reeled around like a compass facing due north. A flap of her daddy's flesh flew from its mouth and landed on her sneaker, before it clumsily stumbled towards the flight attendant.

The lady fearlessly stood upon the upright backs of the exit row seats. Ezra watched the dog leap into the air to destroy the whistling flight attendant.

Like a magician, the Amazing Carmen threw the dog for a loop, wrapping the seatbelt around its thick neck—poof —she disappeared from sight.

After Max was killed, his missing throat mesmerized his wife. It oozed blood from the exposed neck tendons; the emptiness tantamount to his missing face. Buster had all but beheaded her husband.

She felt a strange sense of relief. She wouldn't have to watch Max suffer ever again. Maxine whimpered quietly. Tears flowed down each of her cheeks, connecting at the tip of her heart-shaped chin, before dripping onto her lap. She was perched alone in the empty row next to the window. The intimidating dog stood guard in the row behind her, next to its dead owner. She could hear the dog's heavy breathing and panting. She could smell his bloody dog breath.

The baby started to cry again.

Maxine watched the dog lumber off towards the sound.

Yip...yip...yip! Bruno began rapidly barking and screeching in terror.

"Oh no!" She pulled herself up from her window seat to gain a better vantage.

The big dog stood in the aisle next to the baby, but it

was looking towards the front of the plane to where Bruno was.

Lo and behold, Bruno became a small shooting star of yellow fur, flying down the aisle way. The little dog drifted over the big dog, landing next to her atop Max. With the soft landing on top of flesh, he rolled onto the floor, coming to a rest in a pool of blood that Aunt June had been submerged in. His yellow fur was matted down from slipping through the blackening human fluids.

She darted her eyes to the front of the plane to witness the monster dog deciding which it should kill next. Buster had three choices: the father at the front of coach, who had just tossed Bruno, the crying baby girl, who the dog had already showed interest in, or the beast could choose option three, her loose barking pooch Bruno.

The dog circled its massive frame around to home in on Bruno. It began galloping towards the little dog, bloodied lips flapping with each jolting step, sending saliva tentacles swinging to a jump rope rhyme. Bruno quickly realized the big dog's choice had been made and hightailed it into the first row available. Scurrying into row 13, into the row with the sleeping middle-aged blond woman.

Yip...yip...yip!

Buster landed with a sliding thud next to its deceased elderly master. Turning its body to face the row Bruno had entered. The dog took several Hoover sniffs, one inspecting the air, and the other inhale scanning under the seats.

Then she watched the giant dog become distracted by an upheaval taking place in the front of the coach. Maxine turned her attention to see what the dog had focused on. The African American father was struggling to help his teenage daughter attempt to break into the first-class section; seeking refuge from the brutal massacre happening in coach.

Switching gears, the monster dog turned and bolted towards the doomed father and his young daughter. The dad was leaning over his child, struggling with someone on the other side, so he didn't see the killer dog approaching from behind. The unhinged animal charged the man, but in that moment, the man leaned in closer to swing his meaty fist at someone defending first class. This caused the mad dog to narrowly miss its target. The dog ended up biting into the man's shoulder instead of its intended mark; the man's neck for the kill shot.

"Arrrrrrgh," the man thundered in agony.

Maxine watched the dad dropping to the floor, with the dog clamped tightly to the upper back side of his body. She could see him struggling on his knees to get away, his faded black shirt quickly saturating with his blood. He was fighting the dog with his fists, awkwardly punching at his own back, where the dog had latched on. His eyes wild with fear. The man's daughter gave up on her attempts for safe passage into the blockaded section. She stood motionless, surveying the gruesome scene playing out at her too big feet, and awaiting her own fate.

Maxine could hear the man's fists punching, as he grunted, struggling with the overpowering dog.

The Pitbull was growling viciously.

The bone rattling sound of an Aztec death whistle screamed from behind her.

Whewwwwww!

Maxine twisted back to find the sound's source. Carmen, the flight attendant several rows behind, was squatting atop the seat backs. She balanced on her bare feet, with her body leaning lightly against the storage compartment above. She appeared to be hovering above the dog's owner. Carmen wore a passenger's neck pillow, decorated with fishing lures, duct taped around her neck. Her manicured nails held a noose.

Maxine's mouth dropped wide open as she watched Carmen put two French tipped fingers between her lips and whistled again, *Whewwwww!*

The giant dog stopped its mauling to look for the chilling high-pitched sound, ripping one last chunk of muscle, fat, and t-shirt from the man on the ground. The dog glared up at the flight attendant with its remaining hostile amber eye.

A fierce snarl contorted its face before it barreled towards Carmen. Maxine noticed the dog was off balance from the missing eye and what appeared to be an injured front leg. Tromping over the pile of bodies it slipped through the blood puddles, before landing next to its owner's flowered corpse. The dog struggled to stand, before awkwardly repositioning itself to leap into the air and tackle Carmen from her perch. With the impeccable timing of a skilled cowboy lassoing a bull, Carmen wrapped the safety demonstration seatbelt around the dog's neck, falling backwards from the seats into the row behind, dragging the end of the seatbelt with her. The thick strap became taut around the giant dog's neck. The dog struggled to find its footing. Grappling with her slight body weight that held tightly to the strap from behind the seat. Buster was scrambling in his attempts to make her release the death grip on the seatbelt, biting and snarling at the air around it, jerking its head back and forth. It was the ultimate game of tug-of-war. He wheezed and struggled for a breath.

Then, Maxine watched as the dog began to gain its footing on the aisle seat. Its claws were ripping at the seat's upholstery. Snapping its wide jaws to bite down on the headrest seat cushion. Buster then used his neck strength to pull his body up onto the seat.

It was like fishing Maxine thought.

"Don't let the line have any slack!" Without thinking the words flew from her pink glossed lips.

The dog was building momentum. Its back toes gripped the upholstery, as it crawled its body weight onto the seat, relieving the tension that had been suffocating it. Maxine watched the dog take deep gagging breaths. His good eye bulged from the pumping oxygen.

Carmen was still pulling with all her ability, but her small frame had dropped to the ground when the dog propelled its weight towards her. She jerked back pulling the strap harder. This caused the seat belt noose to slip into the space between the two seats. The entire line went slack. Maxine was sure the dog was going to jump over the back of the seats and kill the flight attendant.

Carmen began reeling the belt strap, rapidly from the back side of the seat, wrenching it until she came eye to eye with the crazed Pitbull. They were staring at one another between the crack in the seat back cushions, its one good, yellow eye was only inches from Carmen's own terror-filled, mascaraed eyes. Maxine could see the dog gasping for breath against the flight attendant's face. It wheezed in its attempt at a growl—creating an ironic whistle. The unnerving struggle of its flailing claws scratched at the seat.

Maxine smelled the iron scent of blood permeating off the animal. Carmen yanked the seatbelt strap down harder. The massive dog could not pull away. Its legs kicked at the air for what seemed like an eternity. And then its struggle was finished.

Maxine could see the monster dog's tongue fully

extended from its mouth, one eyeball hanging by an optic string, and the other bulging from the strangulation. Capped in gore, the massive dog had stopped moving.

Maxine started to tweet out for Bruno, looking for tiny bloody paw prints to lead her to him.

"Come here little pumpkinhead," Maxine sang. "Come to mama.

"THE DOG IS DEAD!" The flight attendant declared to the horrified passengers.

It was as if the plane had been holding its breath as one. Passengers started crying and shouting with relief. They clapped together for getting to live another day. Ezra watched the flight attendant tuck her shirt into her navy-blue skirt, stepping over the flowered corpse of the dog's owner, her bare feet squishing into the blood-soaked carpet. Carmen quickly reached to the floor and collected the Glock 45 lying next to the old woman's head. She placed the gun on top of the cart. As professionally as possible she slipped over the top of the seats to access the rear side of the cart. Unlocking its wheels, she began pulling the cart towards the rear galley. The mauled male flight attendant's body that had been leaning against it flopped to the floor. Carmen kept pulling it, taking quick backward, barefoot steps to the rear of the plane.

People watched as the horror unfolded in front of them. The stage curtains opening to provide a full show of the slaughter that until that moment had been hidden by the trolley.

Passengers began screaming. The flight attendant looked to the massacre she had unwittingly exposed. The people were not screaming at the murderous surprise she had revealed, but instead had become discombobulated at the movement coming from row 15.

"FUCK ME!" Carmen sputtered.

Ezra's saw the dog's mutilated face, yanking back on the seat belt noose wrapped tightly around its neck. Buster began to drag himself upright and dislodge the seat belt from the crack between the seats, where it had become wedged. The momentum from pulling on the noose caused the dog to topple back into the aisleway, its body slumping down next to its owner.

Buster was alive and Carmen had just granted him access to the rear of the plane.

The *birdie* woman was rising from the floor of row 13, where she had been looking under the seats for her loose terrified dog. The old lady's corpse was all that separated *birdie* from the fully breathing, revived, killer dog. The maniac animal was looking directly at the small woman hovering among the pile of dead bodies.

Out from under the seats, stepping between its owner and the mad dog, furious, bloodied Bruno materialized, growling most intimidatingly. The Pomeranian's entire fur coat was as puffy as a ruthless cotton ball.

The flight attendant swiveled her stance. Thrusting her tiny hip into the cart to propel it at a full run towards the rising devil dog. The cart rammed into the male flight attendant Nicco's body, and with a giant shove she capsized the metal box over his corpse, where it landed pinning both Nicco's body and the silver *pit* to the aisle floor. The dog let out an anguished cry from the weight of the trolley. It began struggling to pull its way out from under the heavy box; filled with beverages, soda cans, plastic cups, coffee and napkins, strewn about the brutal massacre.

This flight would be to the death.

Ezra saw that the gun had been catapulted up the aisle from the beverage cart collapse. The weapon now rested near the dead boy—out of reach. The dog continued to struggle to gain its freedom from under the weighted trap, snapping its teeth and jerking its body about in spasms. The flight attendant spotted the old woman's silver elephant-handled cane. Crawling over the cart she was able to reach for the weapon laying on the floor in Aunt June's row. The rabid dog was only a foot from her, with its gruesome fangs repeatedly snapping at her face. Buster kept lunging his upper torso at the flight attendant—just missing her. Grabbing the walking stick, Carmen pulled it close to her chest. She balanced on top of the tipped cart to apply an extra one hundred and ten pounds of weight and keep the dog from wriggling out. Raising the cane high above her head she came down with all her strength. The pointed tip made a cracking sound as it connected with the dog's brick skull— then she repeated again and again—until the dog's face resembled sangria's burgundy citrus pulp. It was no longer recognizable as a dogface. She tossed the cane to the side when she was sure the dog was dead.

The flight attendant slipped her body off the cart and immediately B-lined it to the back of the plane.

"Please stay in your seats!" She demanded the passengers over the intercom. "This is Carmen your flight attendant speaking. The dog has been terminated."

Raising her intonation, she chanted into the speaker, "If

there is a doctor or nurse on board the flight PLEASE press the call button now!"

Ezra watched from the other end of the plane as the heroine, Carmen, pulled a bag out of the compartment above the last row, near the toilets. She then rushed with the large bag in her arms to the front of the plane to assist the hurt passengers in rows seven through fifteen—those who had survived.

"Daddy can we drive back to Las Vegas?"

He didn't answer. He moaned and squeezed her hand.

"I remember what disorder I have daddy...*aviophobia*...a fear of flying."

"The dog has been terminated!"

The senator heard the flight attendant announce the slaying of the dog over the intercom.

He didn't want to come out of the bathroom. During his time spent in the enclosed safe space, he felt his intoxication begin to dissipate, followed by an all-consuming shame for his earlier actions. He wanted to avoid facing the women who had witnessed his behavior; assisting with beating an airline flight attendant unconscious—he was sure that was a federal offense—as well as helping defend the first-class section at the peril of his fellow passengers.

He needed to figure out how he was going to play the story to the press. Of course, the media would be waiting on the tarmac for the plane's arrival. He knew his name would be plastered across the news channels. This could impact his campaign positively or negatively depending on how the media decided to portray him.

"Bad publicity is better than no publicity," a friend had once told him.

The senator wasn't so sure if he needed any more bad

publicity, especially with his name wrapped in the recent women's health care controversy.

He felt the impact of the airplane as it set down on the runway, listening to the squealing of the wheels and the screeching brakes pulling the plane to a slow crawl along the tarmac. He was jarred about in the tight bathroom, banging his elbows against the sink and the wall, while trying to keep from slipping on to the urine stained floor.

"Please stay in your seats until I give the okay to exit the airplane," the captain directed the passengers.

The senator waited for the plane to stop taxiing before he stood from his coward's position on the toilet. He faced his reflection in the mirror. The unfamiliar image returned to him a man rumpled with drops of blood staining his shirtfront and sleeve cuffs from the flight attendant's bleeding nose. He pushed the water faucet and lukewarm water ran over his shaking hands. He smoothed his wayward blond hair down. He couldn't do anything about his glassy red eyes from crying and drinking too much alcohol.

He realized he had forgotten to pray to God.

God was the senator's business as a politician. All fundraising luncheons included a prayer. In each speech he made sure to include God or Jesus at least twice.

"God's blessing has been on Florida from the very beginning, beginning with the Spanish conquistadors...and I believe God isn't done with Florida yet. I believe in Florida. I believe in Palm Beach! I believe in the power of millions of courageous conservatives to make Florida great again."

He carried a Bible in his briefcase. He had a sticker of

the Ichthys, or the Jesus fish, on the back of his Mercedes Benz. He brought his lovely wife and two pint-sized blond girls, dressed alike in perfect petticoat dresses and patent leather Mary Jane sandals, to the Crossroads Mega Church on Sundays. He would bribe the girls with the church's state-of-the-art technology: Bible apps, Christian rock music performances, active youth ministries, a playground and skatepark, but mostly with sprinkled chocolate donuts offered after service. He prayed to God every Sunday; for no more school shootings, for the hurricanes to spare Florida, and for the rising waters to slow down—at least until the next election was over.

After church one Sunday, he stood next to several influential church members, while his diminutive daughter nibbled on her donut; chocolate sprinkles fell on her dress and stuck to the corners of her rosy lips.

"Grace tell us...how was Sunday school today?" A parishioner inquired of the little blond girl.

She took her time and finished chewing her chocolate bite, swallowed it with a gulp, before informing the audience, "You sure got to have a big imagination to believe all that!"

If God could forgive his little girl for questioning her faith, and embarrassing her father, then God would surely forgive him for making a mistake too. Mustering all his will, he unclicked the lock to show vacant on the bathroom door and stepped into the airplane cabin.

The woman with the tortoise shell glasses gave him a look of condemnation. The tattered stewardess was slumped in the seat behind the pissed-off woman, with her concussed head nodding off her shoulder. Drool pouring from her mouth. Blood had crusted to her nose, lips, and chin, and had run down her white shirt. In the back row the senator could see that Derek was peeking through the curtain, ascertaining the economy class' misfortune. Next to Derek, the pretty young woman who had snuck through a break in the wall grimaced with her sultry red lips. She arched her back with her eyes pinched shut from the pain. The senator slinked back to the seat next to Stacy.

She looked at him with pity.

"I suggest you separate yourself from that Derek Beeman guy," Stacy said. "It wouldn't look good for the campaign if people knew that you would align yourself with a man who beat a flight attendant unconscious and potentially helped a Pitbull massacre innocent people would it?"

Out the window, the senator could see the media waiting, as well as the police, and the strobe lights flashing on the waiting ambulances lined up on the tarmac. His heart was racing. He was going to be crucified.

"Oh yea, I forgot," Stacy said. "I quit."

The doors swished open from the galley area and emergency crews came rushing onto the plane.

"What's this food warmer doing here?" One of the uniformed men asked about the forged wall. "Help me get it out of the way!"

The senator watched Derek stand up and take the other end of the cart, assisting the EMT by pushing it to its rightful spot in the galley. Another EMT began helping the injured young woman in the heeled boots. Derek returned from the galley, taking the aisle seat next to the senator. They waited with the other first-class passengers for the plane doors to open.

"So are you still interested in the Miami Vice speedboat ride this afternoon?" Derek asked the senator.

"Who are you?" The senator looked at Derek with blank bloodshot eyes, as if he had never seen him before. "And why would I ever want to go anywhere with you?"

FRIENDLIEST DOG IN THE WORLD

BARBERELLA'S BELLY fat shimmied when the plane set down on the runway. She kept her eyes closed. She had been in a deep sleep, finding no reason to open them, until the plane completed its taxi to the gate.

She waved to the audience with her beauty pageant hand curl, her long blond tresses flowing over her perky breasts, barely hidden by a shiny red, high-sided swimsuit. A white satin sash covered her chest 'Miss Texas 1992.' The announcer wearing a tuxedo, placed a zirconia crown for a queen on top of her head. People cheered. A girl handed her a bouquet of red roses.

The faint sound of the captain's voice droned on, keeping her from her happy place...far far away from reality.

"Won't he just shut up?" She groggily tugged her noise-canceling earphones from her head.

The voice of the captain belted over the speaker but was

drowned out by the sound of people yelling. The chaotic chatter was totally unexpected. The acrid metallic smell of blood had penetrated the airplane through the recycled air system. It was her first sense that something was amiss. Barberella dropped the headphones onto the middle seat and stretched her neck to inspect the pandemonium.

"Please remain in your seats until I tell you that it's okay to exit the airplane," the captain directed passengers. "First and most importantly, we need you to stay seated while the emergency response crews board the plane to assist those who were injured. First they need to remove the passengers needing medical assistance."

Barberella heard people screaming, "Let me off!"

"Leave your personal carry-on luggage and any bags on the plane," the captain explained. "Airline staff will collect your bags and carry-on items after you have exited the plane. The emergency slides will deploy at each of the exit points after the doors have opened. I know this is a stressful situation. Please remain seated until the emergency crews have evacuated the injured. We are asking first class passengers to exit through the front and coach passengers to exit through the back of the plane."

Barberella pulled her substantial weight up by using the seat in front of her. She surveyed the scene with astonishment. On the aisle floor next to her, lay a massive dog strangled by a seat belt, and then apparently pummeled to a pulp by the bloody cane that lay abandoned next to it. Behind the gore that was his face, she could see one eyeball hanging by a thick vein and the dog's tongue fully extended and purple from strangulation.

Barberella was familiar with the telltale signs of strangulation.

During those two years at the ranch following the
divorce, she tried to focus on self-improvement by watching
workout videos, circuit training with five-pound weights in
the family room and taking time to glide on her elliptical
trainer for twenty minutes every afternoon.

Each day she would awake by the rooster's crow. For
breakfast she ate two over easy eggs (from her own chickens)
on buttered toast, challenging herself to not let a single drip
of the thick orange yoke drop on the plate...just for fun. She
would scoop up the third fried egg, still warm in the pan,
flipping it with the spatula into Pumpkin's dog bowl. After
breakfast the big white Pyrenees would follow her to the
stable to feed the horses and chickens. Every morning she
would greet her horse Toby with a carrot before their daily
horseback ride, where they would head west to the hills
beyond the ranch. The horse was a Palomino beauty with
warm brown eyes, a golden coat, with a white mane and a
matching tail.

"Toby is of direct lineage to the 1960's TV horse star
Mr. Ed, whose real name was Bamboo Harvester,"
Barberella bragged to anyone who ever met the horse.

Pumpkin had made a bad habit of straying on the rides,
breaking his own trails, or getting caught by the scent of
wild animal tracks. He would especially run off during the
hunting season; the poor dog would go ballistic at the sound
of gunshots, so she kept him close to her, and leashed him
during the fall. Barberella donned a bright orange hunting
vest and a cozy orange beanie covering her long blond hair
to help keep safe from the hunter's bullets. She wrapped the
dog's long lead around the horn of the saddle, with
Pumpkin running on her left. They walked and trotted at a

slow pace, so to not tire Pumpkin out. She listened to the rhythm of Toby's hooves clomping against the dry earth. Lifting her face to the sky above, she stretched her neck back to take in the sun's rays. As she soaked in the warmth, she watched two red-tailed hawks dancing and soaring above the chilly clear blue sky. The three of them were having such a good time. She felt content in the moment. Sucking up the cool day like an ice pop, after the sweltering Texas summer.

She decided to take the long way returning home. The trail had been worn down from their habitual rides. It looped around a recently mowed alfalfa pasture, and then trailed along a rocky outcropping. Ten minutes later, the rocky area opened to an abandoned field that had returned to its former grassland; with desert patches of prickly pear cactus and large agave plants, the trail disappeared into the tall yellow grass.

Her horse Toby spotted movement on his right side. She noticed it also. And then she heard the rattle of the snake. The Texas Diamond-Back rattler, nestled in a bed of dry grass, was raising its body to expose its diamond scales, hissing with its split tongue, its body had coiled into a strike position. The horse whinnied and stomped his feet before rearing back; knocking her from the saddle, she landed on her posterior with a thud. The wind escaped her as she struggled to catch her breath.

"Where's the snake?" She gasped.

Her blue eyes were wide open, darting back and forth, making no sudden movement. About ten feet away, she saw the snake slithering through the tall grass, heading away from her. Where was her horse, she wondered, propping herself up to look around?

"Oh my God...no!" Barberella rasped.

"Pumpkin!"

Standing to her feet she began running towards Toby. She could see the horse bucking and whinnying on the far side of the field. She stopped. Gasping for air with her hands on her knees. Bolting forward again, her cowboy boots pounding the dry earth. When she approached him, Toby continued to run and buck wildly, with Pumpkin hanging by a noose around his neck. The dog's leash connected him, like the Grim Reaper's umbilical cord, to the frantic horse's saddle. It took nearly half an hour for her to calm the spooked Palomino.

Pumpkin was dead. When she pulled his lifeless body from the knot around the saddle horn—she realized she hadn't fully abandoned hope—at least not until that moment.

Next to her row, Barberella viewed the bodies piled on top of one another, strewed about bloodied and mauled; a scene straight from a Hitchcock horror film.

How much Xanax did I take?

Barberella smacked her face with the palm of her hand.

"Wake up!" She berated herself over the rumblings of the other passengers.

She looked across the aisle, one row up, at a petite bird-like woman primped in blue, fluttering about the dead. Her blood-stained yellow dog was running free, trampling over the bodies, making tight circles around the woman, all the time *yapping*.

"Excuse me lady?" She called for the *little bird's* attention.

The woman looked up, with tear-stained cheeks, and smiled at her.

She clapped her hands together and chirped, "You're alive!"

Yip...yip...yip!

Barberella brushed her thinning, long, blond hair between her fingers nervously. She looked two rows back to see the flight attendant was leaning over a bloodied man. His body rested on the floor, under the seats, with his giant cowboy booted legs splayed into the hallway.

"Hang on Stewart," the flight attendant called to the man. "Help will be here in just a minute."

An older man and a zit-faced teenager from the rear came forward to help pull the drink cart out of the aisleway. Doing their part to help emergency personnel reach the injured. As the heavy metal box was lifted, it revealed the smashed killer dog's mangled body, entangled with the bloodied flight attendant.

Up front, a black man's battered form was stretched across the front of coach. His young daughter was assisting him by soaking up the blood with the blankets she had pulled from the storage space above their seats.

She watched as a handsome face peeked out from the curtains separating first class to survey the scene. She watched his face drop to disgust, and then horror, before slyly letting the curtain fall back in place.

"The flight attendant killed the dog," the *little bird* tweeted in a singsong voice.

Barberella felt the plane come to a complete stop. Less than a minute later, she heard the galley maintenance and food delivery doors on both ends opening. She looked out the round windows to see the ground support was using a dolly to lift the paramedics and emergency crews onto the plane. The solo remaining flight attendant immediately directed them to the front of coach, where the most severely wounded needed tending to.

The paramedics started with the cowboy named Stewart. Several men crawled between the seats in order to maneuver the sizable man from his tight hiding spot on the floor. They were able to roll him onto a stretcher, and then two strong uniformed men quickly carried him out the back of the plane to the waiting ambulance, passing the mortified passengers waiting to deplane. Barberella could see the big man looked jaundiced from his loss of blood, but his quick thinking might have saved him. He had wrapped his leather belt securely around the severed arm to form a tourniquet and slow the blood loss.

The emergency team that entered from the first-class galley struggled to break down the wall. It took precious time to remove the food warmer that had been used by the first-class to divide the plane. She heard the luggage tumbling down around them, with emergency crews finally opening the curtains.

They attempted to revive the concussed flight attendant, so that she could be removed gingerly from the airplane.

One of the medical team began to assess the injured young woman, clad in knee-high black boots. The paramedic, like a shoe salesman, unzipped the tall black boot to evaluate her injuries. Her thin leg exposed—the outside seemed uninjured—the pain on her face showed the inside to be broken. The paramedic lightly twisted the ankle and she cringed. Then he pulled at her big toe. Her face turned to shock like he had zapped her with buzzer prank.

Another EMT checked the critically injured dad's pulse,

before several strong uniformed men carried him off on a stretcher. The large man moaned with each jolting step taken by his rescuers. His skinny daughter followed the medical personnel through the curtains, passing through first-class, out the galley exit to the waiting emergency vehicles.

Additional federal officers and airline workers boarded the plane to help assist passengers to begin the disembarking process via the emergency slides. A swishing sound came from the airplane exit doors opening, and then for several seconds Barberella heard a loud category five hurricane, thundering from the air compressors that blew the emergency slides open.

"Evacuate, Evacuate, Evacuate," the captain's voice came over the speaker.

"Single file please," a federal officer yelled to the hectic passengers. "Please remain calm. Hey! Don't push each other."

The passengers were shoving one another towards the exit points. Looking out the far window she might have believed adults were having fun at the park, their screams looked like smiles, as they slipped down the giant yellow inflatable slides.

"We have a dog pile!" An airline worker called back to the line of waiting passengers. "Please wait for the person in front of you to stand up at the bottom of the slide before you take your turn. Next. Cross your arms in front of you. Next."

Looking out the window she could see the handsome yuppy from first-class was speaking with law enforcement, before he reluctantly turned around with his arms behind his back, so they could handcuff him.

A few rows in front of her, a police officer was

attempting to coerce a young mother holding a baby to follow him off the plane.

"I can't leave him alone," she wept into the infant's pink blanket, hugging the small bundle tight to her chest.

"I'm sorry we need to clear the plane...let's move lady," the officer guided her towards the front.

Barberella listened to the young mother's sobs becoming louder, as she kept looking back at the pile of dead passengers on the aisle floor. Barberella spotted a tiny foot in a red Converse shoe, and a dimpled miniature hand sticking out from under a red headed man, who was half buried by another man with the gray ponytail.

"Mam, please stay where you are!" A young police officer surprised her when he addressed her loudly.

Barberella felt punch-drunk, as she became part of the gruesome nightmare that surrounded her. It was as if she had shown up late for a horror movie.

"I'm going to assist you, so you don't corrupt the crime scene. You are right in the middle of it."

Barberella grabbed her leather Coach purse and started to reach her hand out to the young officer for assistance.

"Mam, please leave your belongings on the plane," he told her.

"You've got to be kidding me?" She said to the officer. "I need my medication."

He reluctantly agreed to let her take the purse.

"I really can't believe this happened," the officer said, shaking his head in disbelief, as he stared at the mangled dog. "I have a *pit* and it's the nicest dog in the world."

Barberella was busy digging in her purse for a Xanax.

"Please use caution when stepping over the bodies mam."

Barberella lifted her leg, taking a wide stance, to reach

the other side of the large elderly woman. Then she started to sidestep past the deceased male flight attendant—her leather flats squishing in his blood.

"Mam, please don't slip," the officer requested.

A disheveled flight attendant was standing in the exit row, her head bowed, next to the dead attendant's body.

"I'm glad you're okay," the woman's unnerved voice addressed Barberella.

Barberella read her name tag, Carmen.

"Carmen, I hear you saved the plane..." the bitter middle-aged woman said to the hero flight attendant, "...and you killed the dog."

As she waved her arms at the bloody scene, and using her fingers, Barberella counted four dead bodies remaining.

"It appears the skies weren't so friendly after all."

Barberella slung the dingy Coach purse over her shoulder, and sashayed to the back of the plane, her hips bumping the seats as she passed.

"Hey Carmen," Barberella turned her body to face the flight attendant just before taking the plunge. "Welcome to The Dog Killer Club."

THE VIBRATING of Dee's iPhone buzzed her from a deep sleep. Her hung-over body was torsioned into a cushy chair. The alarm had been set for 1pm in the afternoon. It had been hours since Dee dropped dead asleep on the leather chair in the Starbucks coffee shop. Uncurling her body, she stretched her arms into the air. Her back popped. Her armpits released a pungent odor from her hangover and no shower. She felt crusty, as she picked the boogers from the corners of her eyes. She blew into the crook of her arm to reveal stank breath. Dee still had to wait thirty more minutes for her rescheduled flight to Miami to depart.

The gate agent guaranteed there would be no dogs on the next flight. The agent hadn't given her an upgrade for her trouble, as she had hoped, in fact the nasty woman gave her a middle seat. Then she proceeded to tell her that she was lucky she even got on, because it was a full flight.

Dee looked at her now cold coffee; the cream had coagulated from sitting on the table next to her for nearly four hours. She had fallen asleep before getting to enjoy the caffeine beverage. Maybe the barista would heat it back up for her.

The barista was helpful, and with her warmed coffee and a fresh outlook on her day, Dee started towards the gate to catch her flight to Miami. Standing on the moving walkway, sipping her drink, she noticed people were gathering around the television screens running CNN and FOX news. Some people held their hands over their mouths, aghast from the information being fed to them; others released groans, while many of the waiting passengers began to cry and murmur about something. *What the fuck was going on?* At her gate she looked up at the television screens broadcasting a real-life horror scene.

"Flight 982 is now being evacuated, having undergone a brutal massacre by an out of control canine during the flight, killing at least four people on board...maybe more. The critically injured are now being taken to Mercy Hospital," the young male reporter revealed.

The screens showed live streaming images of ambulances and police cars with lights flashing, medics running about. The flat screens were transmitting the chaos that had taken over the passengers, as they were tended to on the tarmac. The video panning to show the released airplane emergency slides. Dee watched a plump blond, middle-aged woman, awkwardly sliding down the inflated escape, clutching her purse tightly to her chest.

"This really makes people question if airlines prioritize the safety of passengers," the reporter opinionated.

Dee was pretty sure it wasn't the Pomeranian in the kennel who was responsible for the killings. She shivered thinking of the big service dog's smiling face. The friendly dog had even waved at her with his white paw.

The television displayed the image of a flight attendant

being escorted by a paramedic to the waiting ambulance; blood was crusted to her broken nose. Then the screen clipped to an African American man, bloodied on a gurney, his mouth open with misery. His young daughter held his hand by his side. Seeing the girl, made her to think about the small freckle faced boy she had returned the toy airplane to. He had told her it was his lucky day. She hoped he was okay.

"Florida Senator Mike Young was on board the doomed flight. It is being reported that he helped numerous passengers to the safety of the first-class section. Fending off the savage dog with suitcases and quote, "A will to survive.""

A photo mug shot filled the screen. It showed a dog eerily similar in appearance to the giant silver one she had met earlier on the plane; the photo flashed a nearly identical Pitbull with a white chest, white paws, and cropped ears.

"We were just informed that the killer dog was of the American Pitbull Terrier breed. As you know these animals have received a lot of grief from the press over the years. I'm sure this won't help the breed's plight. In being fair and balanced in my reporting...I will say...I have a Pitbull myself and it is the nicest dog in the world. In addition, in all fairness, I am reporting facts...you are more likely to be bitten by a Chihuahua than a Pitbull."

Dee thought about being bit by either animal.

The woman standing next to her chimed in, "I'd rather be bitten by a Chihuahua any day."

The reporter interrupted the woman with more breaking news.

"We have just learned the dog was a trained Diabetic Alert Service Animal. Um. I imagine the dog trainer will have some explaining to do. In addition, we are being told the out of control animal was euthanized. I'm sorry to say the dog's owner did not survive the mauling. The names of those who sadly perished aboard Flight 982, in this tragedy over Miami, will be released once family members have been notified. Hold on...here...we have someone who was on the flight."

"Mam, could you please tell us what happened today?"

The reporter was addressing a petite woman dressed in blue, holding a blood soaked, shit-covered, semi-fuzzy, yellow Pomeranian.

"The butcher's name was Buster," she flitted off the screen. "The flight attendant saved us all."

"Butcher who? Mam?"

"I was supposed to be on that flight," Dee crossed her arms in front of her chest, when she spoke to the woman standing next to her.

"Wow," the woman looked at her surprised. "Well I guess it's your lucky day!"

Seven months before the Freedom Flight 982 massacre...

I'm alerted by the sound of knocking at the front door. Anticipating anything to be behind it.

Knock-knock-knock.

I'm sitting as still as a cat ready to pounce.

"Hold up," my man Carlos calls out to the person behind the door.

I watch him rise from the couch, where he had been lounging with his tattooed neck cradled by crossed arms behind his head. He turns to our friends Aaron and Roberto; both chilling in the two recliner chairs, playing video games. I can hear the videogame car engines revving, with rapid gunshots blasting from the television speaker.

"Watch these guys," Carlos commands our friends and me. "These *vatos* have been acting sketchy lately."

He cautiously cracks the door to peer out at the visitor.

Opening it all the way, letting loose a stream of sunshine into the dark space. A dry hot draft infiltrates the room's dank air from the running swamp cooler. I see the dust fairies dancing around in the light to form sharp diagonal lines against the dingy room.

The first man, dressed in black jeans and a white t-shirt, enters the house with a limp. I take several subtle inhales, familiar with the smell of marijuana and burritos, both saturating his clothing and skin. The second man struts in displaying a blue bandana under his white baseball cap. The bandana is just like the one Carlos and I wear. Dark sunglasses cover the man's eyes, and I get a whiff of cigarettes and stale whiskey.

"? Hola Carlos...como esta?" The second bandana-wearing stranger asks Carlos how he is.

The bandana man nearly trips over his sneakers, backing up in surprise when he spots me hidden in the corner.

"Miereda...shit...no lo veo."

He reaches his hands out, telling me to stop, even though I hadn't moved. He is joking by displaying this defensive motion. My mouth twists into a grin. He speaks my language. When he sees my big smile, he reaches down towards me and pats my meaty head. I reach my tongue out to grab a quick taste of his hand.

"Buen perro," the first burrito smelling man says, plopping down on a chair near the window, with the shades drawn closed.

I am a good dog.

"Don't touch my dog ese," Carlos cautioned the bandana-wearing man sternly. "You need my permission— otherwise he might kill you."

The bandana man takes off his sunglasses and smiles,

squinting his warm friendly eyes, "¿ El me matara con besos?"

The others in the room laugh at this comment and they are probably right—I would kill him with kisses.

"Joker. El transporte."

Without hesitation, I stand and proceed directly to the bandana man, aggressively pushing him towards Carlos and the kitchen.

"Joker. Heel."

I immediately stop directing the man and return to Carlos's side.

"Joker. Sientate."

I sit.

He rubs my stubby ears and tells me I'm a good dog.

"Joker is a dog of extreme temperament. See how calm and relaxed he is...when I trigger this dog it turns into a killing machine. It only takes one trigger sound for Joker to rip the throats out of every person in this room—starting with you."

"Joker. Place."

I return to my bed in the dark corner next to the front door.

"Let's do business," Carlos says, leading the bandana-wearing stranger to the kitchen.

Our friends Aaron and Roberto stay behind on their recliners, playing the loud video game. The burrito smelling man sits near the window. I am trying to pay attention to Carlos in the other room, but I can hardly hear what he is doing under the game's roaring engines and gunshots turned to high volume.

"How much do you want?" I hear Carlos ask the man.

The clinking and shuffling of items and the wall separating us muffle their voices.

I hear a faint slur of words and "eight ball."

Ball! I love to play with a ball.

Carlos throws the ball in the dirt-covered backyard. I make dust twisters from running so fast. We visit my best dog friends every week. I have my strong friend Redrum; he is pure muscle with a red nose and does all the same protection exercises as me. We get treats for climbing fences and jumping through car windows. People shoot semi-automatic guns while petting me and telling me how good I am.

"Look how calm and relaxed he is bro," Carlos tells his friends, slicking down the raised hackle along my back that formed during the intense exercises.

The people put bite sleeves on their arms, commanding me to "Grip." I lunge at them; biting down on the sleeve, with them swinging me around in circles. When I was younger, they would give me the sleeve to bite down and play with as a reward, but nowadays I am man focused—not equipment focused.

Some days I get to see my little friend Tank, they say she is a Chihuahua. I love her and take naps with her, and let her climb on me, and boss me around; she even steals bones out from under me. I love her sneakiness.

My very favorite days are when Carlos's two kids come to visit. They are as tall as me, one smells sugary and the other tastes salty. I take care of them. They ride me like a *cabella*, after I lick them clean, because they taste as good as they smell.

"Joker you're in charge," Carlos will tell me while laughing. "You're the *niños'* nanny dog."

I would never let anything happen to them. I know bad things happen. I have dealt with bad men before.

I see my friends are smoking the glass pipe with burrito man. The room gets cloudy with the sweet chemical smell. I want to sneeze. I rub my nose into my armpit to stop it. Burrito man peeks through the blinds, squinting into the light, and then lets the slats snap shut. Carlos and the bandana stranger emerge from the kitchen. I watch the burrito man rise from his seat, near the front window, preparing to leave with his companion. The bandana man struts over to the front door, opening it wide. Blinded by the light, everything happens so fast.

Two more men are standing outside the door; they are wearing our same blue bandanas and welding guns. They push past burrito man into the living room. I hear the loud popping of bullets from a gun. I smell the gunpowder. I see Aaron's chest explode, darkening with the sweet metallic smell; he is gagging on the sticky liquid. Roberto's mouth is hanging open in a muted, never-ending scream.

Whewwwwww!

Carlos lets out one long whistle before being shot in the head.

I watch my friend fall directly back. His body slams to the floor from the bullet's impact.

I am already striking, my one hundred and fifty pounds of muscle slamming into the man holding the gun. *Disable.* My mouth clamps onto his arm, forcing him to drop the gun. I'm not letting go. I start shaking his appendage. He is screaming in agony. I can see burrito man reaching for the abandoned gun, now lying on the carpet. I release the man's arm from my mouth, turning to attack burrito man, aiming my bite for his throat. I only get one small nip out of him as he jerks away, running out the front door, holding his oozing neck with his hands.

I give chase, racing through the open front door, into the hot screaming sun of the Albuquerque suburb, to tackle him from behind. He drops onto the dirt yard, with me on top of him, smothering him in the sand. I hear another bullet zoom past. Turning around to face the aggressor, my attention is now aimed at the first bandana man now holding a gun. He is standing in the front doorway of my house. Running towards him, I zigzag to avoid the raining bullets. I count three bullets missing me, minus the earlier shots. I hear the click of the empty weapon. *Kill.* I latch onto his arm with every ounce of strength I have in me. The bandana man is hollering in pain. *Crunch.* His arm breaks in my mouth, my fangs digging deep into his flesh, releasing a gush of blood into my mouth from the mauling. I see his partner, burrito man, being helped along with the other injured man. They get into the dark blue low-rider parked in front. The bandana man is punching me in the face with his good arm; I clamp down with my jaws squeezing even harder, feeling the popping of blood vessels like candy pop rocks in my mouth. He is pulling me, attached to his oozing broken arm, towards the waiting car. Another man steps out of the slow-moving vehicle and begins kicking me. I hear the gun cock.

Bang!

I feel a stinging pain on my hind leg, causing me to loosen the grip. Bandana man pulls out from my bite as he is dragged into the vehicle by his fellow gang members. The engine revs and the car screeches off. I am running after the men. Lunging at the car trunk, attempting to grip the metal with my claws, before tumbling off and hitting my head —hard.

Knocking me out.

My eyes flutter open to find my body stretched across the two yellow lines that run down the center of the road. I shake my beaten skull. Jumping up to take off after the car. I think I see it far off in the distance; dancing in the waves of the desert heat. I sprint as fast as I can, my toenails clicking against the asphalt, my breath on fire. The car keeps moving further away, until it disappears around a corner. I no longer know where I am.

Looking around at the tan suburban stucco houses, each one looks the same, with rocky yards and cactus plants in zero water landscaping. The burning concrete sidewalk pains my feet and I'm so thirsty.

As luck would have it, coming around a corner, an inviting cool green lawn oasis welcomes me. Sprinklers are twisting fresh water to make misty rainbows. I spy two small girls my height playing in the fluid cloud; the children are a bag of biscuits at the end of the rainbow. They smile at me. I smile back.

The End.

If you enjoyed this book
please write a brief **review**
on the site where you purchased it.

ABOUT THE AUTHOR

Cactus Rose Moloney is a freelance writer for newspapers, has worked in public relations, and was once a librarian on the island of Borneo in Southeast Asia. She earned a degree in Journalism and English from Colorado State University. She splits her time between Soldotna, Alaska and Moab, Utah. Her purpose is to scare the crap out of people.